obson, Carmichael, Rufus, Humphrey, Eddie,
eoffrey, Sturgess.

Marshall, Brown, Wood, Rayner, Crispin,
aite, Foster, Morrison.

teacher, Cuthbert, Nicholas, Cyril, Jeremy,
geley (just being sent off).

Nicholas

RENÉ GOSCINNY & JEAN-JACQUES SEMPÉ

Translated by Anthea Bell

Phaidon Press Inc.
180 Varick Street
New York, NY 10014

www.phaidon.com

Reprinted 2006 (twice)
First published in French as *Le petit Nicolas*

ISBN-13: 978 0 7148 4529 6 (US edition)
ISBN-10: 0 7148 4529 9

A CIP catalogue record for this book is available
from the British Library.

Designed by James Cartledge and Phil Cleaver of etal-design
Printed in China

CONTENTS

SCHOOL

A Photograph to Treasure

When we got to school this morning we were all feeling pleased because we were going to have a class photograph taken and it would be a memento for us to treasure all our lives, like our teacher said, and she told us to be sure we were neat and clean and we'd brushed our hair.

My hair was all plastered down with pomade when I arrived in the playground. All my friends were there and our teacher was yelling at Geoffrey for coming in his Martian suit. Geoffrey's dad is very rich and buys him all the toys he wants. Geoffrey was telling our teacher he'd be photographed in his Martian suit or not at all, so there.

The photographer and his camera had arrived too, and our teacher told him to be quick about it or else we'd miss math, and Cuthbert, who is top of the class and teacher's pet, said it would be too bad to miss math because he did like math so much and he'd got all his problems done, and Eddie, who is a very strong boy, wanted to punch Cuthbert's nose, only Cuthbert wears glasses so we can't pound him as much as we'd like to. Our teacher started shouting and saying we were quite impossible and if this kind of thing went on there wouldn't be any photograph at all and we'd go straight in and start lessons. So then the photographer said, "Now, now, now,

just keep calm. Don't you worry, I know exactly how to handle children!"

The photographer decided we ought to be in three rows: one row sitting on the ground, the second row standing up with our teacher sitting on a chair in the middle, and the third row standing on wooden boxes behind them. That photographer really had some fabulous ideas.

We went down to the school basement to get the boxes. We had a great time because it was dark down there and Rufus put an old sack over his head and shouted, "Whooo! I'm a ghost!" Then we saw our teacher coming. She didn't look too pleased, so we went off with the boxes, fast, and the only boy left was Rufus. He couldn't see what was going on because of the sack, so he went on shouting, "Whooo! I'm a ghost!" and then our teacher took the sack off his head and Rufus got a big surprise.

Back in the playground our teacher let go of Rufus's ear and she clasped her head in her hands. "Oh no!" she said. "You're all messy!" I suppose we *had* got a little bit dirty fooling around down in the basement. Our teacher was mad, but the photographer said it didn't matter, and we'd have time to go and wash while he got the boxes and the chair into position for the photo. Apart from Cuthbert the only one whose face was still clean was Geoffrey, on account of his head being inside the Martian helmet which is like a goldfish bowl.

"There, you see?" Geoffrey told our teacher. "If they'd all come in Martian suits you wouldn't have had any trouble." I could see our teacher wanted to pull Geoffrey's ears too, but the goldfish bowl was all smooth so she couldn't. That Martian outfit is really fantastic!

After we'd washed our faces and combed our hair we came back. We were just a bit wet, but the photographer said that didn't matter, it wouldn't show up in the picture.

"Right!" said the photographer. "Now, do you want to please your teacher?" We said yes, we did, because we like our teacher; she's really nice if you don't make her mad. "Very well," said the photographer, "get into your places like good children. Big boys on the boxes, the middle-sized ones on the ground and the little ones sitting." So we started getting into our places, and the photographer was telling our teacher how you can get children to do anything if you just exercise a little patience, but our teacher couldn't stop to hear the end of it. She had to come and separate us, because we all wanted to be on the boxes.

"I'm the only big boy anyway!" Eddie was shouting, and he was pushing everyone else off the boxes as they tried to get up. Geoffrey wasn't giving in, so Eddie hit him on the goldfish bowl and hurt his hand a lot. Geoffrey's goldfish bowl was jammed and it took several of us to get it off.

Our teacher warned us that she was giving us one last chance, and if we didn't behave it would be math, so we decided we'd better keep quiet and we started getting into position. Geoffrey went over to the photographer.

"What's that camera of yours?" he asked.

The photographer smiled and said, "It's a magic box, sonny, and in a minute you'll see the little birdie come out!"

"Gosh, yours is ancient!" said Geoffrey.

"I've got one my dad gave me with a lens hood and a close-up lens and a telephoto lens and masses of different filters..."

The photographer seemed to be surprised, he stopped smiling and he told Geoffrey to go back to his place.

"I suppose you do at least have a photoelectric cell?" asked Geoffrey.

"For the last time, will you get back into position?" shouted the photographer. He seemed very worked up all of a sudden.

We got into position. I was sitting on the ground beside Alec. Alec is my friend who is very fat and who is always eating. Just now he was taking a bite out of a piece of bread and jelly and the photographer told him to stop eating, but Alec said he had to keep his strength up.

Our teacher was sitting right behind Alec, and she snapped, "Put that bread and jelly away!" which made him jump with surprise and he dropped the bread and jelly on his shirt-front.

"There!" said Alec, trying to scrape the jelly off his shirt with the piece of bread. The teacher said the only solution was to put Alec in the back row where the jelly stain wouldn't show. "Eddie, change places with your friend," she said.

"He isn't my friend," said Eddie, "and he's not having my place and all he has to do is turn his back to the camera; that way no one will see the jelly or his great fat tummy either." Our teacher was mad and she punished Eddie by making him do lines by copying – *I must not refuse to change places with a friend who has dropped a piece of bread and jelly on his shirt* – one hundred times.

Eddie didn't say anything, he got down off his box and started out for the front row while Alec started out for the back row. There was a bit of a mix-up, specially when Eddie punched Alec on the nose in passing, and Alec tried to kick Eddie, but Eddie, who can move very fast, dodged it, and it was Cuthbert who got kicked, only luckily not where he wears his glasses. Not that that stopped him bursting into tears and wailing that he couldn't see any more and no one loved him and he wished he were dead. Our teacher comforted him and wiped his nose and combed his hair again and told Alec to write out a hundred times *I must not hit a friend who wears glasses and who is not even trying to hurt me.*

"Good!" said Cuthbert, so our teacher gave him some lines too. Cuthbert was so surprised he didn't even cry. Then our teacher really started handing out the punishments, we all got lots of lines, and finally she said, "Now, suppose you all make up your minds to stand still. If you're very, very good I'll let you off your lines. Right! Stand up straight, smile nicely, and the gentleman will take a lovely photo of us!" Well, we didn't want to upset our teacher, so we did as she said: we all stood up straight and smiled.

Only we never did get that photo to be a memento to treasure all our lives. It didn't come off, because we suddenly found the photographer wasn't there any more. He had just gone away without a word to anyone!

Playing Cowboys

I invited our gang round to my house this afternoon to play cowboys. They brought all their gear. Rufus was wearing the policeman outfit his dad gave him, with the cap and handcuffs and gun and nightstick and whistle. Eddie was wearing his big brother's old Boy Scout hat and he had a cartridge belt with lots of wooden cartridges, and two holsters with revolvers in them, really fantastic revolvers with butts made of the same kind of bone stuff as that powder compact Dad bought Mom after they had their argument about the meat being overdone but Mom said it was all because Dad was late home. Alec was dressed up like a Cherokee, with a tomahawk and feathers on his head, he looked like a big chicken; Geoffrey likes dressing up and he has this very rich dad who gives him anything he wants, and he had a real cowboy suit, with sheepskin chaps and a leather waistcoat, a check shirt, a big hat, and cap pistols and spurs with fantastic sharp points. I had a black mask which I got at a party, and my pop-gun which shoots arrows, and a red hankie round my neck which was really one of my mom's old scarves. We all looked great!

We were out in the garden and Mom told us she'd call us when it was dinner-time.

"OK," I said, "now, I'm the brave young cowboy on my white

horse and you are all bandits, but I win in the end." Only the others objected. That's the trouble, it's no fun playing alone but when you aren't playing alone the others *will* keep arguing.

"So why can't *I* be the brave young cowboy?" asked Eddie. "I want a white horse too!"

"What, you a brave young cowboy with a face like that?" said Alec.

"You shut up, Chief, or I'll give you a kick in the pants, or is it the tail feathers!" said Eddie, who is a very strong boy and usually he prefers punching people's noses so I was surprised about kicking Alec's tail; but he was right, because Alec did look like a big chicken.

"Anyway, I'm going to be the sheriff," said Rufus.

"Sheriff?" said Geoffrey. "Don't make me laugh! Whoever saw a sheriff in a policeman's cap? You'd look silly!"

Rufus, whose dad is a policeman, took offence. "My dad wore a cap when he joined the police and he didn't look silly!"

"Well, he would have done if he'd worn one in Texas!" said Geoffrey, and Rufus hit him, so Geoffrey drew his gun and said, "You'll be sorry for this!" and Rufus hit him again and Geoffrey dropped to the ground going bang! bang! bang! with his cap pistol, and Rufus clutched his belly and made frightful faces and fell down shouting, "Got me, you coyote, but I'll have my revenge!"

I was galloping round the yard hitting my behind to make me go faster and Eddie came up to me and said, "Get off that horse, I'm having that white horse."

"Oh no you're not," I said, "this is my garden and I'm having the white horse!" So Eddie punched my nose and Rufus blew his whistle very loud.

"You're a horse-thief," he told Eddie. "We hang horse-thieves here in Kansas City."

Then Alec came running over and said, "Hold on, *you* can't hang him, I'm the sheriff!"

"Since when?" asked Rufus. Alec isn't all that keen on fighting but he took his tomahawk and whacked Rufus on the head with it, which Rufus was not expecting. Luckily he was wearing his policeman's cap.

"My cap! You've squashed my cap!" shouted Rufus, and then he started chasing Alec while I went back to galloping round the yard.

"Hey, everybody, stop!" said Eddie. "I've got an idea. We're the goodies, and Alec is the tribe of Cherokee, and he tries to capture us and he takes one prisoner, but we arrive and we rescue the prisoner and then Alec is beaten!" We all thought that was a great idea, except for Alec.

"Why do *I* have to be the tribe of Cherokee?" he asked.

"Because of your feathers, idiot!" said Geoffrey, "and if you don't like it you needn't play, you're just being annoying!"

"All right then, I *won't* play!" said Alec, and he went off to sulk in a corner and eat a chocolate croissant he had found in his pocket.

"But he's got to play!" said Eddie. "He's our only Cherokee. Anyway, if he doesn't play I'm going to pluck his feathers!" Alec said OK, he'd play, but only if he could end up being a good Cherokee.

"All right, all right," said Geoffrey. "But honestly, you are *so* irritating!"

"Who'll be the prisoner?" I asked.

"Geoffrey," said Eddie. "We can tie him to that tree with the clothesline."

"That's what you think!" said Geoffrey. "Anyway, I can't be the prisoner because *I've* got better clothes than all of you!"

"So what?" said Eddie. "I'm not saying I won't play just because I've got a white horse, am I?"

"You haven't got the white horse," I said, "*I've* got the white horse!" Eddie got mad and he said the white horse was his and if I didn't like it he'd give me another punch on the nose.

"Just you try it!" I said, so he did.

"Don't move, Oklahoma Kid!" shouted Geoffrey, firing his guns right, left and center, and Rufus blew his whistle and said, "Here, I'm the sheriff, I'm arresting you all!" and Alec hit him on the cap with his tomahawk and said he was taking him prisoner and Rufus was upset because he'd dropped his whistle in the grass and I was crying a bit and telling Eddie this was my yard and I never wanted anything to do with him again, and everyone was shouting and it was all great, we were having a fantastic time.

And then Dad came out of the house. He didn't seem to be too pleased. "Now then, children, what's all this ruckus?" he asked. "Can't you play nicely?"

"Please, it's Geoffrey; he doesn't want to be the prisoner," Eddie explained.

"Want a shove in the face?" asked Geoffrey, and they started fighting again, but Dad separated them.

"Come along, boys," he said. "I'll show you the way to play. *I* will be the prisoner!" We were thrilled. My dad is really great! We tied him to the tree with the clothesline and we'd only just finished when we saw Mr. Billings jump over the garden hedge.

Mr. Billings lives next door and he likes annoying Dad. "I'm playing too!" he said. "I'll be the chief. Standing Bull, that's me!"

"Oh, go away, please, Billings, no one invited you!" said Dad.

Mr. Billings was fantastic, he stood there in front of Dad with his arms folded saying, "Let the paleface hold his tongue!" Dad was struggling like mad to get free, and Mr. Billings started dancing round the tree giving war whoops. We'd have liked to stay and watch Dad and Mr. Billings fooling around playing cowboys, but we couldn't because Mom called us in for dinner and afterwards we went up to my room to play with the electric train set. I never knew Dad liked playing cowboys so much. When we came down later in the evening Mr. Billings had been gone a long time, but there was Dad still tied to the tree, shouting and making faces.

Fancy being able to play games all by yourself! My dad is great!

Old Spuds

Our teacher was not in school today. We were standing on line in the playground ready to go into our classroom when Mr. Goodman, one of the other teachers, came and told us, "Your teacher is away today, she's out sick."

So Mr. Goodman took us all to our classroom. We call him Old Spuds, though not to his face, of course. We call him Spuds because he is always saying, "Boy, look me in the eye!" and potatoes have eyes. No, I didn't get it at first either, it was some of the older boys who explained it to me. Old Spuds has a big mustache and he is very strict; it's no good trying to play him up. So we were sorry he was going to look after us, but luckily when we got into our classroom he said, "I can't stay, I have some work to do with the Principal. Now, boys, look me in the eye and promise to behave." So we all looked him in the eye and promised to behave. We nearly always do behave, anyway.

It's a funny thing, though, Old Spuds didn't seem to trust us. He asked who was top of the class.

"Me, sir!" said Cuthbert proudly. Which was true, Cuthbert is top of the class and teacher's pet and we aren't all that mad about him only we can't hit him much because of his glasses.

"Very well," said Old Spuds, "you can sit at the teacher's

desk and keep an eye on your friends. I'll look in from time to time to see how you're getting on. Now, do some reading." Cuthbert went and sat at the teacher's desk, looking very pleased with himself, and Old Spuds went off.

"We'd be having math now," said Cuthbert. "Get your notebooks out and we'll do a problem." So Matthew asked if he was out of his tiny mind. Cuthbert, who really did seem to think he was our teacher, shouted, "You shut up, Matthew!"

"Come over here and say that to my face, if you dare!" said Matthew, and the classroom door opened and in came Old Spuds, grinning.

"Aha!" he said. "You didn't know I was listening behind the door, eh? You, boy, look me in the eye!" So Matthew looked him in the eye, and I don't know what he saw there but he didn't seem to like it much. "You will write the lines *I must not be rude to a friend who is keeping an eye on me and wants to set me some problems* one hundred times." After that Old Spuds went out, but he promised to be back.

Jeremy suggested keeping a look-out for him at the door, and we all thought that was a good idea except Cuthbert, who shouted, "Jeremy, get back to your place!" Jeremy put his tongue out at Cuthbert and went and stood by the door, looking through the keyhole.

"Anyone there, Jeremy?" asked Matthew, and Jeremy said he couldn't see a thing. So then Matthew got up and he said he was going to make Cuthbert eat his math book, and that was a really great idea, only Cuthbert didn't seem too thrilled about it and he shouted, "No, I've got glasses!"

"Then you can eat your glasses too!" said Matthew, who seemed dead set on Cuthbert having something to eat. But Geoffrey said there wasn't any point in wasting time fooling around and why didn't we play ball?

"But what about our problems?" asked Cuthbert, not looking very pleased, but we took no notice and started passing the ball, and it was great, playing in among the desks. When I'm grown up I'm going to buy myself a classroom just for playing in. And then we heard a screech and there was Jeremy sitting on the floor holding his nose. Old Spuds had just opened the door and Jeremy couldn't have seen him coming.

"What on earth is the matter with you?" asked Old Spuds, very surprised, but Jeremy didn't say anything, he just went on yelling, so Old Spuds scooped him up and took him out. We retrieved our ball and went back to our desks.

When Old Spuds came back with Jeremy, whose nose was all swollen, he said he'd had about enough of this, and if it went on we'd see what we would see. "Why can't you all be like your friend Cuthbert?" he asked. "He is a nicely behaved boy!" And Old Spuds went out. We asked Jeremy what had happened, and he said he'd been hypnotized by the keyhole and dropped off to sleep.

"A farmer goes to market with a basket of eggs," said Cuthbert. "He is selling his eggs for five francs a dozen…"

"It was all your fault I got that bump on the nose," said Jeremy.

"That's right!" said Matthew. "Come on, let's make him eat his math book and the farmer and the basket of eggs and his glasses and all!" So Cuthbert started to cry, and he was saying we were very naughty and he was going to tell our parents and we'd all be expelled, when Old Spuds opened the door. We were all sitting at our desks, not saying anything, and Old Spuds looked at Cuthbert who was sitting at the teacher's desk all by himself, howling.

"Now what?" said Old Spuds. "Are *you* giving trouble this time? Really, this is driving me crazy! Every time I come in I find another of you acting up! Now, all of you, look me in the eye! If I come back and see anything out of the ordinary one more time, I shall deal with you most severely!" And off he went again.

We decided this was not the time to act up any more, because when Old Spuds gets really mad he hands out some pretty nasty punishments. We sat perfectly still and all we heard was Cuthbert sniffling and Alec munching, which is something he does all the time. Then we heard a tiny little noise over by the door, and we saw the door knob turn ever so slowly, and then the door began to open, little by little, with a squeak of its hinges. We all held our breath and watched. Even Alec stopped munching. Then someone suddenly let out a yell: "It's Old Spuds!" And the door opened and Old Spuds came in, bright red in the face.

"Who said that?" he asked.

"Nicholas did!" said Cuthbert.

"You're a liar!" I shouted. "It's not true!" and it was quite true it wasn't true. Rufus had said it.

"You did say it, you did, you did!" shouted Cuthbert and he burst into tears.

"You will be kept in, boy!" Old Spuds told me. So then I burst into tears too and I said it wasn't fair and I was going to run away from school for ever and never come back and then they'd be sorry.

"Please, sir, it wasn't him, sir, it was Cuthbert who said Old Spuds!" cried Rufus.

"I never said Old Spuds!" shouted Cuthbert.

"You did say Old Spuds, I heard you say Old Spuds quite clearly, you did say Old Spuds, Old Spuds!"

"Very well, if this goes on you will all be kept in!" said Old Spuds.

"Why me, sir?" asked Alec. "I never said Old Spuds!"

"I don't want to hear that ridiculous nickname any more, understand?" said Old Spuds. He seemed really upset.

"I won't be kept in!" shouted Cuthbert, and he rolled about on the floor crying and he got hiccups and first he went red in the face and then he went blue. Practically everybody in the class was shouting or crying by now, and I thought Old Spuds was about to start too when the Principal came in.

"What in the world is going on, Sp… Mr. Goodman?" asked the Principal.

"I haven't the faintest idea, sir," said Old Spuds. "I've got one of them rolling about on the floor, and another getting a nosebleed when I open the door, and the rest of them yelling – I never saw anything like it in all my born days!" And Old Spuds ran his hands through his hair and his mustache was quivering like crazy.

Next morning our own teacher was back, but Old Spuds was away, out sick.

A Game of Soccer

Alec asked a whole lot of our gang from school to meet him this afternoon at the vacant lot not far from where we live. Alec is my friend who is fat and he likes eating, and the reason he was fixing up a soccer game was because his dad had given him a brand new soccer ball and we were going to have a really great game. Alec is OK.

We met at the vacant lot at three o'clock, eighteen of us. First we had to pick two teams.

Choosing the referee was easy enough: we all picked Cuthbert. Cuthbert is top of the class and we're not crazy about him, but we can't hit him because he wears glasses, and all that is a pretty good combination for a referee. Anyway no one wanted Cuthbert on their team because he's not much good at sports and he cries so easily. However, we ran into a spot of difficulty when Cuthbert said he needed a whistle, and the only person who had a whistle was Rufus, whose dad is a policeman.

"I'm not lending him my whistle. It's a family heirloom," said Rufus, and that was that. Finally we decided that Cuthbert would tell Rufus when he wanted the whistle blown and then Rufus would blow it for him.

"Well, are we going to start or not? I'm getting really hungry," said Alec.

But now things were tricky, because if Cuthbert was ref there were only seventeen players for the teams and that meant odd numbers. Then we found the answer: someone would be linesman and wave a little flag every time the ball went out of play. We chose Max. One linesman isn't much to keep an eye on the whole pitch, but Max can run very fast because he's got long thin legs with big dirty knees. Max didn't want to be linesman, he wanted to play, and he said anyway he didn't have a flag. All the same, he finally agreed to be linesman for the first half and wave his hankie for a flag, though it wasn't a clean hankie, but of course when he came out he didn't know it was going to be a flag.

"Right, let's get on with it!" said Alec.

It was easier now, because there were only sixteen players. We needed two captains, one for each team. The only thing was, everyone wanted to be captain, except for Alec who wanted to be in goal because he doesn't like running. That was OK, because Alec is a good goalie. There's so much of him he covers a lot of the goal mouth. However, that still left us with fifteen captains, which was several too many.

"I'm the strongest, so I ought to be captain!" shouted Eddie. "And if anyone says no I'm going to punch his nose!"

"I've got the best soccer uniform, so I'm going to be captain!" shouted Geoffrey, so Eddie punched his nose.

Geoffrey was quite right, though, he did have the best uniform; his rich dad had bought him a complete soccer player's outfit, with a red, white, and blue striped shirt.

"I'm going to be captain!" shouted Rufus. "If I'm not captain I will get my dad and he'll put you all in jail!"

I had the idea of tossing a coin for it. Well, tossing two coins, because the first one got lost in the grass and we couldn't find it. Jeremy had lent the coin and he wasn't too pleased about losing it; he went on searching, even though Geoffrey promised that his dad would send him a check for the same amount. Finally two captains were chosen: Geoffrey and me.

"Listen, I don't want to be late for dinner!" yelled Alec. "Are we starting or aren't we?"

Next we had to form our teams. That went off all right except for Eddie. Geoffrey and I both wanted Eddie, because when he's got the ball no one ever tackles him. Not that he plays all that well, but everyone is afraid of him. Jeremy suddenly found his coin and cheered up, so we asked him if we could borrow it again to toss up for Eddie, and we lost it again. Jeremy was really annoyed this time and he went back to searching while we drew straws with blades of grass. Geoffrey got Eddie. Geoffrey said Eddie could be goalie, because he thought no one would dare come anywhere near the goal then, let alone put the ball in. Eddie loses his temper very easily. Alec was sitting down in between the sticks which

marked out his goal, not looking too pleased. "Well, *now* what about it?" he shouted.

So we got into position. It wasn't all that easy, because we were only seven a side, not counting the goalies, and there was a lot of arguing on both sides. Most people wanted to be center-forwards. Jeremy wanted to be right back, but that was because his coin had dropped somewhere around there and he wanted to carry on looking for it while he played.

Geoffrey soon got his side straightened out, because Eddie punched a lot of people and then they got into position without any more trouble, rubbing their noses. Eddie punches pretty hard!

We couldn't get my team to settle things, though, till Eddie said he'd come and punch our noses too. So then we got into position.

"Whistle!" Cuthbert told Rufus, and Rufus, who was on my team, blew the whistle for kick-off.

But Geoffrey still wasn't happy. "Here, we've been tricked!" he said. "The sun's in our eyes. I don't see why my team has to have the worst end!"

I told him if he didn't like the sun all he had to do was close his eyes and very likely he'd play better that way, so then we had a fight. Rufus started blowing his whistle.

"I never told you to whistle!" shouted Cuthbert. "I'm the ref!" Rufus got cross and said he didn't need Cuthbert's permission to blow his whistle, he'd blow his whistle when and if he felt like it, so there! And he started whistling like crazy.

"You're naughty, you're *really* naughty!" shouted Cuthbert, beginning to cry.

"Oh, for goodness' sake!" said Alec, in his goal.

But no one took any notice. I was still fighting Geoffrey, and I'd torn his nice red, white, and blue shirt, and he was saying, "Yah, yah, yah! Doesn't matter! My dad will buy me lots more!" and he was kicking my shins. Rufus was chasing Cuthbert, who was shouting, "I've got glasses! I've got glasses!" Jeremy wasn't doing anything to anyone, he was looking for his coin, but he still couldn't find it. Eddie, who'd been waiting patiently in his own goal, got fed up and started punching the noses closest to him, which happened to belong to his own side. We were all shouting and running around and we were having a really fabulous time!

"Stop it, will you?" Alec shouted again.

Eddie lost his temper with Alec. "You were in such a hurry to play, weren't you?" he said. "Right, so we're playing! If you've got anything to say, save it for half-time!"

"What do you mean, half-time?" asked Alec. "I've only just noticed – we haven't got a ball! I left it at home by mistake."

The Inspector

Our teacher was distracted when she came into the classroom. "There's an inspector at school today," she told us. "Now, I can count on you boys to behave yourselves and make a good impression, can't I?" We all promised to behave, and anyway she didn't need to worry because we nearly always do behave.

"The thing is, he's a new inspector," our teacher said. "The old one was used to you, but he's retired now..." And then she gave us lots and lots of advice. She told us not to speak without being spoken to, not to laugh without permission, not to drop marbles like last time the old inspector came when he ended up flat on the floor, and she asked Alec not to eat things while the inspector was there, and she told Matthew, who's bottom of the class, to try to be inconspicuous. Sometimes I wonder if our teacher thinks we're complete idiots. Still, we're fond of our teacher, so we promised to do what she said. She looked round to see if the classroom and all of us were nice and neat and clean, and she said the classroom was neater than some among us. Then she asked Cuthbert, who is top of the class and teacher's pet, to put ink in the inkwells in case the inspector wanted to give us some dictation. So Cuthbert got the big ink bottle and he was about to start filling the inkwells in the front desk where Cyril and Jeremy sit when someone

shouted, "Here comes the inspector!" Cuthbert jumped so much he spilt ink all over the desk. It was only a joke, the inspector wasn't there at all and our teacher was very annoyed.

"I saw you, Matthew!" she said. "It was you who played that silly trick. Go and stand in the corner!" Matthew started to cry, and he said if he stood in the corner he wouldn't be inconspicuous and the inspector would ask him lots of questions and he didn't know the answers and he'd cry, and it wasn't a silly trick, he *had* seen the inspector, crossing the playground with the Principal, so because that was quite true our teacher said OK, that's enough for the time being. The trouble was that the front desk was covered with ink, so our teacher said we must put it in the back row where no one would see it. We started moving it, and that was a lot of fun because we had to move all the other desks too, and we were having a really terrific time when the inspector and the Principal came in.

We didn't have to stand up because we were all standing up anyway, and everyone looked very surprised. "These are the little boys, they're … er … they're a bit scatter-brained," said the Principal.

"I see, I see," said the inspector. "Well, sit down, boys." So we all sat down, and Cyril and Jeremy had their backs to the blackboard because we'd turned their desk round while we were moving it. The inspector looked at our teacher and asked whether these two pupils always sat that way round. Our teacher's face went like Matthew's when people ask him questions, but she didn't cry.

"We – we had a slight accident," she said. The inspector didn't look too pleased. He had great big bushy eyebrows very close to his eyes.

"Discipline, that's what is called for," he said. "Come along, boys, put that desk back in place." So we all stood up and the inspector shouted, "No, not all of you, just you two." Cyril and Jeremy turned the desk round and sat down. The inspector smiled, and rested his hands on the desk top. "Very well," he said, "and what exactly were you up to before I arrived?"

"Moving this desk, sir," said Cyril.

"Never mind the desk!" said the inspector, who was looking rather worked up. "And in any case, *why* were you moving it?"

"Because of the ink," said Jeremy.

"Ink?" said the inspector, and he looked at his hands, which were blue all over. The inspector heaved a sigh and wiped them on a handkerchief.

We realized that the inspector and our teacher and the Principal didn't look as if they were having any fun, so we decided to be very, very good.

"I can see you have problems keeping order," the inspector told our teacher. "A little elementary psychology is all you need!" And then he turned to us with a great big smile and his eyebrows shot up in the air. "Now, children, I want to be friends with you! You mustn't be afraid of me. I know you like a bit of fun – why, I like a good laugh myself! Did you ever hear the joke about the two deaf men? One deaf man says to the other: 'Are you going fishing?' And the other deaf man says, 'No, I'm going fishing.' 'Oh,' says the first one, 'I thought you were going fishing.'"

It's a pity our teacher had told us not to laugh without permission, because we could hardly restrain ourselves. I'm going to tell my dad that story when I get home this evening, because he'll like it and I'm sure he hasn't heard it before. The inspector laughed a lot, but then he didn't need anyone's permission. However, when he saw that the whole class was quite quiet he put his eyebrows back into place and coughed and said, "Well, that's enough joking. Now for some work."

"We were studying fables," said our teacher. "They were learning the story of *The Crow and the Fox*."

"Excellent, excellent!" said the inspector. "Carry on as usual." Our teacher pretended to be picking someone out of the class at random, and then she pointed to Cuthbert.

"Cuthbert, will you tell us the story?" she said. But the inspector raised his hand.

"If I may?" he said to our teacher, and then he pointed to Matthew. "You at the back there, tell me the story of *The Crow and the Fox*." Matthew opened his mouth and started to cry.

"What on earth is the matter with him?" asked the inspector, and our teacher said he must please excuse Matthew, Matthew was very shy. So Rufus got asked instead. Rufus is one of our gang and his dad's a policeman. Rufus said he didn't know the story by heart but he knew more or less what it was about, and he started explaining that it was the story of a crow who had some Roquefort cheese in his beak.

"Roquefort?" asked the inspector, looking more surprised every minute.

"No, it wasn't Roquefort," said Alec. "It was Camembert."

"Oh no it wasn't," said Rufus. "He wouldn't have Camembert in his beak because it's runny and it smells awful, so there."

"It might smell awful," Alec said, "but it's terrific to eat, and anyway, soap smells good but it tastes awful. I tried it once."

Rufus said, "Yah, you're just stupid, and I'm going to tell my dad to give your dad lots of parking tickets." And then they had a fight.

Everyone jumped up and started shouting, except Matthew, who was still sitting crying in his corner, and Cuthbert, who had gone up to the blackboard and was telling the story of *The Crow and the Fox*, and our teacher and the Principal were shouting, "Silence!" We all had no end of fun.

When it was over and we were all sitting down the inspector took out his handkerchief and wiped his face and got ink all over it, and it was a real shame we weren't allowed to laugh, because it wasn't going to be easy to control ourselves till playtime.

The inspector went over to our teacher and shook her hand. "Dear lady, you have my deepest sympathy," he said. "I never appreciated before what a true vocation our profession is! Carry on the good work! Keep a stiff upper lip! Well done!" And he left in a great hurry, along with the Principal.

We're really very fond of our teacher, but honestly, she was terribly unfair! It was all because of us the inspector said such nice things to her, and she went and kept us all in after school!

Rex

When I came out of school today I followed a little dog down the road. He looked lost and he was all on his own and I felt very sorry for him. I thought that little dog would be pleased to have a friend, and I went to quite a lot of bother to catch him. He didn't seem to be all that keen on going home with me, I expect he wasn't sure he could trust me, so I gave him half my chocolate croissant and he ate it and started wagging his tail like crazy and I called him Rex, like a dog in a crime movie I saw last Thursday.

After eating my chocolate croissant almost as fast as Alec could have done (Alec is my fat friend who's always eating) Rex followed me home quite happily. I thought he would be a nice surprise for Mom and Dad. And then I'd teach him tricks, and he could be our watchdog, and help me catch crooks like in that movie last Thursday.

You'll never believe this, I bet, but when I got home Mom wasn't particularly pleased to see Rex. In fact she wasn't at all pleased. I suppose some of it was Rex's fault really. We went into the sitting room and Mom came in and kissed me and asked if I'd had a good day at school and not done anything silly and then she saw Rex and started screeching, "Where did you find that animal?" I started to explain that he was a poor

little lost dog who was going to help me arrest lots of crooks, but instead of keeping still Rex jumped up on an armchair and started biting the cushion. It was the armchair where Dad isn't allowed to sit unless there are visitors, too!

Mom did some more shouting, and she said she had forbidden me to bring animals into the house – which was true, she did say that the time I brought a mouse home – and she said it was dangerous, this might be a rabid dog and he'd bite us all and we would all start frothing at the mouth and she was giving me one minute exactly to get that dog out of the house.

I had a spot of trouble persuading Rex to let go of the cushion, and even then he kept a bit of it in his mouth. I don't see how he could possibly like the taste of it. Then I went out into the garden, carrying Rex. I felt like crying, so I did cry. Maybe Rex felt sad too, but I don't know, he was too busy spitting out little bits of wool from the cushion.

Dad came home and found us both sitting outside the door, me crying and Rex spitting. "Well, well!" said Dad. "What's going on here?" So I explained how Mom didn't want Rex and Rex was my friend and I was the only friend he had in the world and he was going to help me catch crooks and he'd do tricks for me and I was very unhappy. And I started crying some more while Rex scratched one ear with his back foot which is a very difficult thing to do – we tried it once at school and the only one who was any good at it was Max because of his long legs.

Dad patted me on the head and then he said Mom was right about it being dangerous to bring strange dogs into the house because they might not be well and they might bite you and then you'd all start foaming at the mouth and going crazy, and as I would learn later on at school, Pasteur, who was a great benefactor of humanity, invented some medicine to cure it but it's most unpleasant all the same. So I told Dad that Rex was perfectly well and he liked eating things and he was ever so intelligent. And then Dad looked at Rex and tickled him under the chin as he does to me sometimes.

"He does seem to be a healthy little creature," said Dad, and Rex began licking his hand. Dad liked this no end. "He's sweet!" said Dad, and he put out his other hand and said, "Come on, give us a paw then!" and Rex shook paws and then he licked Dad's other hand and then he scratched his own ear, and one way or another he was keeping very busy. Dad was enjoying himself. "Right," he told me, "you wait here and I'll try to fix it with your mother." And he went into the house. Dad is great! While Dad was fixing it with Mom I played with Rex. He started to beg but as I didn't have anything to give him he went back to scratching his ear. Rex was fantastic!

When Dad came out of the house he didn't look as pleased as before. He sat down beside me and patted my head and told me Mom wouldn't have Rex in the house, especially not after that armchair business. I thought of starting to cry but then I had an idea. "If Mom doesn't want Rex in the house we could keep him in the yard," I said. Dad thought a moment and then he said

that was a good idea as Rex couldn't do any damage in the yard. We'd make him a dog house right away. I hugged Dad.

We went up to the attic to find some planks and Dad got out his tools. Rex started to eat the begonias but that didn't matter as much as the living room armchair because we've got more begonias than armchairs.

Dad began choosing planks. "You just wait, we'll make him a really fine dog house!" he told me.

"And then we'll teach him lots and lots of tricks and he can be a watchdog," I said.

"That's right," said Dad. "We could teach him to chase off intruders, like Mr. Billings." Mr. Billings is our neighbor and he and Dad like to annoy each other. We were having a great time, Rex and me and Dad! It wasn't so good when Dad let out a yell because of hammering his finger and Mom came outside.

"What on earth are you doing?" asked Mom. So I explained how Dad and I had decided to keep Rex in the yard where there aren't any armchairs and Dad was making him a dog house and Dad was going to teach Rex to bite Mr. Billings so Mr. Billings would go mad. Dad didn't say much, just sucked his finger and looked at Mom. Mom was not a bit pleased. She said she didn't want that animal staying here. "And just look what he's done to my begonias!" Rex raised his head and went up to Mom wagging his tail and then he begged. Mom looked at him and then she bent down and patted Rex's head and as Rex licked her hand there was a knock at the garden gate.

Dad went to open the gate and a man came in. He looked at Rex and he said, "So there you are, Kiki! I have been looking for you everywhere!"

"May I ask what you want?" asked Dad.

"What do I want?" said the man. "I want my dog! Kiki here ran away while I was taking him for his walk, and I was told some ragamuffin had been seen bringing him this way."

"He isn't Kiki, he's Rex," I said. "And we're both going to catch crooks like in that movie last Thursday and we're going to train him to annoy Mr. Billings." Only Rex was looking very pleased and he jumped into the man's arms.

"How do I know this dog is yours?" said Dad. "He's a stray."

"What about his collar?" said the man. "Didn't you notice that? It's got my name on it, J.J. Temple, and my address. I could sue you, you know! Come along, poor little Kiki. There, there, there!" And the man went off with Rex.

We all just stood there rooted to the spot, and then Mom started to cry. So Dad comforted Mom and he promised her I'd bring another dog home one of these days.

Jocky

We had a new boy at school yesterday. Our teacher came into the classroom in the afternoon with a little boy and she said, "Now, boys, I've got a new friend for you. He comes from abroad and his parents are sending him to this school to learn our language. I expect you to help me. You must all be very nice to him." And she said to the new boy, "Tell your little friends your name." The new boy didn't understand what our teacher was saying, he just smiled, and so she told us he was called Jochen van der Velde, and wrote his name on the board.

"Ja, Jochen," said the new boy.

"Please, miss," asked Max, "is it really Yocken or Jochen?" Our teacher explained that his name was spelt "Jochen" but in his own language it sounded like "Yocken."

"OK, we'll call him Jocky," said Max.

"No, you have to say Yocky," said Jeremy.

"You shut up, Yeremy," said Max, and our teacher sent them both to stand in the corner.

Our teacher gave Jocky the desk next to Cuthbert. Cuthbert looked as if he didn't like the new boy much; he's top of the class and teacher's pet so he's always scared of new boys in case they get to be top of the class and teacher's pet instead. Cuthbert knows he's safe enough with us.

Jocky sat down, still grinning. "It's a pity no one can speak his language," said our teacher. "I know the rudiments of Flemish," said Cuthbert. You've got to admit it, Cuthbert can use some pretty long words. But after Cuthbert had said his rudiments of Flemish to Jocky, Jocky just looked at him and then he started laughing and he tapped his forehead. Cuthbert was very cross, but Jocky was right. We found out afterwards that Cuthbert had been telling him a load of old rubbish about the yard of his uncle which was bigger than the pen of his aunt. Cuthbert is nuts!

The bell rang for playtime and we all went out, except for Jeremy, Max and Matthew, who had detention. Matthew is bottom of the class and he hadn't done his homework properly. When Matthew gets asked questions he always has detention.

Out in the playground we all gathered round Jocky. We asked him lots of questions, but all he did was grin. Finally he started talking, but we couldn't make head or tail of it, it was just a lot of jabber. "The trouble is he's using the original sound track," said Geoffrey, who goes to the movies a lot. "What he needs is subtitles."

"Maybe I can translate," said Cuthbert, chomping at the bit to try out his rudiments again.

"Huh!" said Rufus. "You're a loony!" The new boy liked this. He pointed at Cuthbert and said, "Ah! Loony, loony, loony." He seemed awfully pleased with himself. Cuthbert went off crying; Cuthbert's always crying. We were beginning to like Jocky, and I gave him a piece of my chocolate.

"What games do they play in your country?" asked Eddie. Of course, Jocky didn't understand. He went on saying, "Loony, loony, loony."

But Geoffrey said, "That's a really ridiculous question! They play soccer, of course."

"I didn't ask you, you great fat nitwit," said Eddie.

"Great fat nitwit! Loony, loony!" said the new boy. He seemed to be enjoying himself a lot. But Geoffrey took offence at Eddie's tone.

"Who's a great fat nitwit?" he asked, which was a mistake, because Eddie is very strong and likes punching people's noses so Geoffrey's nose got punched. When he saw the punch Jocky stopped saying "Loony" and "Great fat nitwit" and looked at Eddie and said, "Ah! Good!" And he put up his fists and started dancing round Eddie like the boxers on Matthew's television. We don't have one yet but I do wish Dad would buy one.

"What's the matter with *him?*" asked Eddie, and Geoffrey, still rubbing his nose, said, "He wants a boxing match with you, you fool!"

"Right!" said Eddie, and he squared up to Jocky. But Jocky was ever so much better than Eddie and he got in so many hits that Eddie began to lose his temper. "How am I expected to punch his nose if he won't keep it still?" he said, and then bam! Jocky gave Eddie a punch which made Eddie fall down. Eddie didn't mind. "Hey, you're darned good!" he said, getting up. "Darned good, loony, great fat nitwit!" said the new boy. He was a really fast learner. Then playtime was over, and as usual Alec was complaining he hadn't had time to finish the croissants he'd brought to school.

When we got back into the classroom our teacher asked Jocky if he'd had a nice time, and Cuthbert got up and said,

"Please, miss, they're teaching him rude words!"

"That's a dirty lie!" said Matthew, who'd stayed in at playtime.

"Loony, great fat nitwit, dirty lie!" said Jocky proudly.

We kept quiet, because we could see our teacher was not at all pleased. "You should be ashamed of yourselves," she said. "Taking advantage of a boy who doesn't know your language! And after I asked you to be nice to him, too! I can see you're not to be trusted; you've behaved like disgusting little savages!"

"Loony, great fat nitwit, dirty lie, disgusting little savages!" said Jocky. He looked awfully pleased to be learning so much.

Our teacher stared at him with wide round eyes. "Er… Jochen, dear," she said. "We don't say things like that!"

"You see, miss? What did I tell you?" asked Cuthbert.

"Cuthbert, if you don't want to be kept in after school I suggest you keep your comments to yourself!" said our teacher, and Cuthbert started crying. "Sappy little nimrod!" said someone, but our teacher couldn't find out who it was or I'd have been punished, and then Cuthbert rolled about on the floor sobbing that nobody loved him and everything was horrible and he was going to die and our teacher had to take him out to bathe his face and calm him down.

When she came back with Cuthbert she was looking very tired, but luckily the bell went for the end of school. Before she left the room our teacher looked at the new boy and she said, "Whatever are your parents going to think…?"

"Sappy little nimrod!" said Jocky, shaking hands with her.

Our teacher was wrong to worry, though. Jocky's parents must have thought he'd learnt all he needed.

We could tell that, because Jocky didn't come back to school any more.

LOONY!
GREAT FAT NITWIT!
DIRTY LIE!!...

A Bunch of Flowers

It was my mom's birthday and I decided to buy her a present like every year since last year (before that I was too little).

I took all the money out of my piggy bank and luckily there was a lot because quite by chance Mom had given me some the day before. I knew what I was going to get her for a present: an enormous huge bunch of flowers to put in the big blue vase in the living room.

I could hardly wait for school to be over so I could go and buy my present. I kept my hand in my pocket all the time at school so as not to lose my money, even when we were playing soccer at playtime – but since I wasn't in goal that didn't matter. Alec is our goalie. "Why are you running about with one hand in your pocket?" he asked me. I explained that I was going to buy my mom some flowers, and he said personally he'd rather have something to eat, like a cake or some candy, but since the present wasn't for him I took no notice and I got a ball past him into the goal. We won 44–32.

When we came out of school Alec went along to the flower shop with me, eating half the chocolate croissant he'd saved from the grammar lesson. We went into the shop and I put all my money on the counter and told the lady I wanted an enormous huge bunch of flowers for my mom, only no begonias because we had plenty of those in our garden, so it wasn't worth buying any more. "We want something nice," said Alec, and he went and stuck his nose into the flowers in the window to see how they smelt. The lady counted my money, and she said she was afraid she couldn't give me a *very* enormous bunch of flowers. I was very sad, so the lady looked at me and thought for a moment, and then she told me I was a dear little boy and she patted me on the head and said she'd fix it. She picked out all sorts of flowers, and she put in a lot of green leaves. Alec liked them, because he said they looked like nice fresh vegetables. It was a big bunch, really fantastic; the lady wrapped it up in crackly transparent paper and told me to be careful how I carried it. So now I had my big bunch of flowers and Alec had finished smelling the others in the window, and I said thank you to the lady and we went out.

I was feeling very pleased with my flowers when we met Geoffrey, Matthew and Rufus from school.

"Hey, look at Nicholas!" said Geoffrey. "He looks a real nimrod with that bunch of flowers!"

"You're jolly lucky I'm carrying these flowers or I'd whack you!" I said.

"Give them to me," said Alec. "I don't mind holding them while you whack Geoffrey." So I gave Alec my bunch of flowers, and Geoffrey whacked me. We had our fight, and then I said time was getting on, so we stopped. However, I had to wait a bit longer, because Matthew said, "Just look at Alec – now *he* looks a real nimrod holding a bunch of flowers!" So Alec hit him over the head with the bunch of flowers.

"My flowers!" I shouted. "You'll hurt my flowers!" I was right, too. Alec went on hitting Matthew with the bunch and the flowers were flying all over the place because the paper was torn, and Matthew was shouting, "Doesn't hurt, yah boo, doesn't hurt!"

By the time Alec stopped, Matthew's head was covered with greenery and Alec was right, he did look like something you could cook for Sunday lunch. I started picking up my flowers and I told my friends they were beastly. "That's right!" said Rufus. "You shouldn't have gone and done that to Nicholas's flowers!"

"Nobody asked you!" said Geoffrey, and they started whaling on each other. Alec had gone home, because the sight of Matthew's head made him feel hungry and he didn't want to be late for dinner.

I went off with my flowers. Some of them were missing, and there was no more greenery or paper left, but it was still a nice bunch. Then, a little further on, I met Eddie.

"Hi," said Eddie, "have a game of marbles?"

"I can't," I said. "I've got to get home and give my mom these flowers." But Eddie said it was still quite early. And I like playing marbles – I'm good at marbles, I just take aim and wham! I nearly always win. So I put my flowers down on the pavement and I started playing with Eddie, and it's great playing marbles with Eddie

because he often loses. The trouble is he doesn't like losing and he said I was cheating and I told him he was lying, so he shoved me and I sat down on top of my bunch of flowers and it didn't do them any good.

"I'm going to tell Mom what you did to her flowers," I said to Eddie, and Eddie was very upset. He helped me pick out the least squashed ones. I like Eddie, he's OK.

I started off again. My bunch wasn't very big any more, but the flowers I did have left were all right; one of them was just a bit squashed, but the other two were fine. Then I saw Jeremy on his bike.

I decided I wasn't going to fight him, because if I went on fighting all my friends I met in the street I soon wouldn't have any flowers at all left to give Mom. Anyway, it's none of their business if I want to give my mom some flowers. I've got a perfect right to give her flowers, and personally I think they're just jealous because Mom would be very pleased with me and give me something nice for dessert and tell me what a kind boy I am, so why do they all want to gang up on me anyway?

"Hi, Nicholas!" said Jeremy.

"Right nimrod yourself!" I shouted back. "So what's the matter with my bunch of flowers, then?"

Jeremy got off his bike and looked at me in surprise and said, "What bunch of flowers?"

"This bunch of flowers!" I said, and I threw the flowers in his face. I don't think Jeremy was expecting to get a faceful of flowers, and anyway he didn't like it. He threw the flowers into the road and they landed on the roof of a passing car and drove off with the car.

"My flowers!" I shouted. "My mom's flowers!"

"Don't worry!" said Jeremy. "I'll follow the car on my bike." Jeremy's OK, but he doesn't pedal very fast, specially not uphill, even if he says he *is* training to win the *Tour de France* when he's grown up. When he came back he said he hadn't been able to catch up with the car, there was a lot of traffic and it had got away from him, but he did bring me back one flower which had fallen off its roof. Unfortunately it was the squashed one.

Jeremy rode off very fast – it's downhill all the way to his house – and I went home with my crumpled flower. I had a big lump in my throat. Like when I bring home my report card with my monthly report and it's got all zeros on it.

I opened the door and I said, "Happy Birthday, Mom," and then I burst into tears. Mom looked at the flower; she seemed a bit surprised. Then she put her arms round me and hugged me lots and lots of times, and she said it was the nicest bunch of flowers she'd ever had, and she put the flower in the big blue vase in the sitting room.

I don't care what you say, my mom is OK!

Our Report Cards

This afternoon was no fun at all, because the Principal came into our classroom to give out the report cards with the monthly scores they give us at our school. He didn't look too pleased when he came in with the report cards under his arm. "I have worked in the field of education for years," said the Principal, "and never before have I known such an idle class! Your teacher's remarks on your reports speak for themselves! I will now give out the report cards." And Matthew started to cry. Matthew is bottom of the class, and every month our teacher writes lots of things to his mom and dad on his report card, and Matthew's mom and dad are cross and say he can't have any dessert or watch television. Matthew told me they've got so used to it by now that once a month his mom doesn't bother to make a dessert at all and his dad arranges to go next door to watch television.

On my report card it said: "A rowdy and often inattentive pupil, given to fighting his friends. Could do better." Rufus's said: "Will persist in playing with a whistle in class; I have frequently had to confiscate it. Could do better." The only one who apparently couldn't do better was Cuthbert. Cuthbert is top of the class and teacher's pet. The Principal told us we ought to follow Cuthbert's example, we were a disgrace, and we'd all end up in jail which would be a very sad thing for our mothers and fathers who undoubtedly had other plans for us. And then he went out.

We weren't very happy, because our dads are supposed to sign our report cards and it can be a rather trying moment. So when the bell went for the end of school, instead of running for the door as usual and pushing and shoving and throwing book bags at each other, we filed out very quiet and glum. Even our teacher was looking sad. We don't hold any grudges against out teacher. I suppose we did play up a bit this month, and Geoffrey oughtn't really to have poured his inkwell all over Jeremy who had fallen down making horrible faces because Eddie had punched his nose when actually it was Rufus who'd been pulling Eddie's hair all the time.

Out in the road we didn't go very fast, in fact we were dragging our feet. We stopped outside the baker's to wait for Alec, who had gone in to buy six little chocolate croissants, which he started eating right away. "I've got to stock up," said Alec, "because of no dessert tonight..." and he heaved a big sigh, still munching. Alec's report card had said: "This pupil would be top of the class if he put as much effort into his work as he does into eating. Could do better."

Eddie was the one who seemed least worried. "I'm not scared!" he said. "My dad won't say a thing. I just look him straight in the eye and then he signs the report card and that's that." Eddie has all the luck! When we got to the corner we all went different ways. Matthew was crying as he walked off,

Alec was eating and Rufus was blowing his whistle in a very subdued way.

I was left with Eddie. "If you're frightened to go home, I can fix it," said Eddie. "You can come back with me and stay the night at our house." Eddie is OK. We went along together while Eddie explained how he looks his dad straight in the eye. But the closer we got to Eddie's home the less Eddie talked, and by the time we arrived at the door he wasn't saying anything at all. We waited a moment, and then I said to Eddie, "Well, do we go in?"

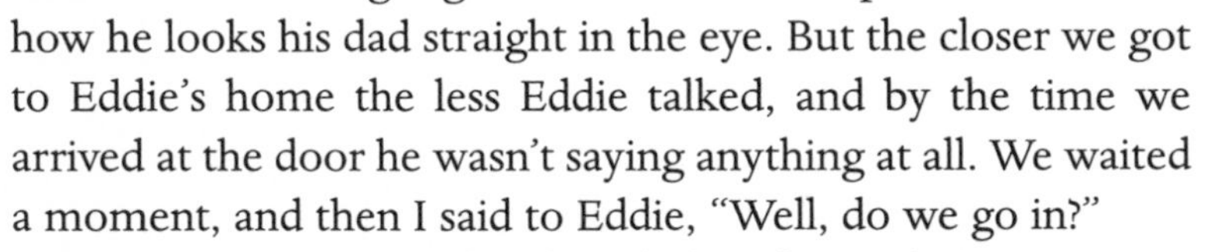

Eddie scratched his head and then he said, "Hang on a moment. I'll come back for you." And Eddie went into his house. He left the door open a crack, and I heard a slap and a loud voice saying, "No dessert for *you* tonight, you lazy little good for nothing," and then Eddie crying. I guess Eddie couldn't have looked his dad quite straight enough in the eye.

The trouble was I had to go home myself now. I started walking, taking care not to tread on the cracks between the paving stones, which was easy because I was going slowly. I knew just what Dad would say. He'd say he had always been top of the class at school himself, and his own father was extremely proud of my dad, and he had brought home lots of cups and certificates of merit from school, and he wishes he could show them to me but they got lost when he and Mom were married and he moved house. And then Dad would say I'd never get anywhere in life, I would be poor, and people would say, "Oh, that's Nicholas who got such bad scores at school!"

and they'd all point and laugh at me. After that Dad would tell me about all the sacrifices he was making to give me a decent education that would set me up for life, and how ungrateful I was and I didn't even mind about the grief I was causing my poor parents, and I wasn't having any dessert tonight and as for going to the movies, well, we'd wait and see when I next got my report card.

Dad would say all those things to me, just like last month and the month before, but I'd had enough. I'm going to tell him how unhappy I am, I thought, and if that's how he feels, right, I'm running away from home, a long way away, and they'll miss me very much, and I won't come back for years and years and years, and by then I'll have lots of money and Dad will be ashamed of telling me I'd never get anywhere in life and no one will dare point or laugh at me, and I will spend my money taking Mom and Dad to the movies, and everyone will say, "Ooh, look, that's Nicholas who has lots of money, and he's paying to take his mom and dad to the movies even though they were so unkind to him," and I will take our teacher and the Principal to the movies too – and then suddenly I was at home.

What with telling myself all these super stories, I'd forgotten about my report card and walked very fast. I had a big lump in my throat and I told myself perhaps it would be best to leave right away and not come back for years and years and years, only it was getting dark and Mom doesn't like me to be out late. So I went in.

Dad was in the living room talking to Mom. He had a whole lot of papers on the table in front of him, and he wasn't looking pleased. "The amount of money that gets spent in this house is quite incredible!" Dad was saying. "Anyone would think I was a multimillionaire! Just look at these bills! The butcher's bill! The grocer's bill! Oh, yes, and I'm the one who has to pay for it all!" Mom wasn't looking pleased either, and she was telling Dad he had no idea of the cost of living, and some day he ought to go shopping with her, and she had a good mind to go home to her mother and they oughtn't to discuss such matters in front of little Nicholas. Then I gave my report card to Dad, and Dad opened it and signed it and gave it right back to me saying, "This has nothing to do with little Nicholas. All I ask is for someone to explain to me why a leg of lamb should cost that much!"

"Nicholas, go up to your room and play," said Mom.

"That's right, you just run along," said Dad.

I went up to my room and lay down on the bed and I started to cry.

If my mom and dad loved me at all, they'd take just a little bit of notice of me! They would!

Louise

I wasn't too pleased when Mom told me one of her friends was coming for tea and bringing her little girl. I don't like girls. They're sappy, they only play at dolls and going shopping, and they're always crying. Well, I suppose I sometimes cry myself, but only for something serious like when the living room vase got broken and Dad told me off and it wasn't fair because I didn't do it on purpose and anyway it was an ugly vase and I know Dad doesn't like me to play soccer in the house but it was raining outside.

"You must be nice to Louise," said Mom. "She's a dear little girl, and I want you to show her what good manners you have."

When Mom wants me to show what good manners I have she makes me wear a blue suit and a white shirt and I look a proper nitwit. I told Mom I'd rather go to the movies with our gang and see the Western they were showing, but Mom gave me that look of hers which means she's not standing for any nonsense.

"And you are not to be rough with little Louise, or you'll have me to deal with, understand?" Mom told me. So at four o'clock Mom's friend arrived with her little girl. Mom's friend hugged me and said oh, what a big boy I was, like people always do, and then she said, "This is Louise." Louise and I took a look

at each other. Louise had yellow hair in braids, blue eyes, and her nose and her dress were red. We shook hands, very quickly. Then it was tea-time, and that was OK, because when people come for tea there's chocolate *gateau* and you can come back for another slice. During tea Louise and I didn't say anything much, just ate without looking at each other. When we'd all finished Mom said, "Well, children, run along and play. Take Louise up to your room and show her your nice toys, Nicholas." Mom had a big smile all over her face, but she was still giving me that look which means she's standing no nonsense.

Louise and I went up to my room, and I didn't know what to say to her. Louise started it, she said, "You're all dressed up like a monkey!" That annoyed me, so I said, "Well, you're only a sappy girl!" so then she whacked me. I felt like crying, but I didn't because Mom wanted me to show what good manners I have, so I pulled one of Louise's braids instead and she kicked my shin. I couldn't help letting out a yell then, because it hurt. I was going to whack Louise back when she changed the subject.

"How about these toys of yours?" she asked. "Are you going to show me?" I was about to tell her they were boys' toys when she spotted my teddy bear, the one I shaved half the fur off with Dad's razor. I only got half of it shaved because the razor packed up. "Gosh, do you play with dolls?" said Louise, and she began laughing. I was just going to pull one of her braids again and she was just going to hit me, when the door opened and both our moms came in.

"Well, having a nice time, children?" asked Mom.

"Ooh, yes!" said Louise, opening her eyes wide and fluttering her eyelashes. Mom hugged her and said, "She really is adorable! Such a dear little chicken!" and Louise put in some more work with her eyelashes.

"Show Louise your nice books!" said my mom, and the other mom said we were *both* dear little chickens, and they went out.

I took my books out of the cupboard and gave them to Louise, but she didn't look at them, just dropped them on the floor, even the one about cowboys which is terrific. "I don't like silly old books," said Louise, "haven't you got anything that's more fun?" And then she looked in the cupboard and found my red plane, the good one with an elastic band which makes it fly.

"Leave that alone," I said, "that isn't a girl's toy, that's my plane!" and I tried to get it back. But Louise dodged me.

"I'm the guest," she said, "I've got the right to play with all your toys and if you say I can't I will fetch my mom and then we'll see!" I didn't know just what to do, I didn't want her to break my plane but I didn't want her fetching her mom either because that would mean trouble. So while I was thinking, Louise was turning the propeller to wind up the elastic, and then she let go of the plane and it flew out of the window.

"Now look what you've done!" I said. "You've lost my plane!" And I started to cry.

"Don't be ridiculous, your plane isn't lost!" said Louise. "Look, it came down in the yard. We'd better go and get it."

We went down into the sitting room and I asked Mom if we could go out to play in the garden, and Mom said it was too cold, but Louise did her eyelash trick again and said she did so want to see the pretty flowers. So then Mom said what a dear little chicken she was and told us to wrap up well

before we went out. I'll have to learn that eyelash trick, it does seem to work wonders!

Out in the yard I picked up my plane, luckily it was all right, and then Louise said, "What shall we do now?"

"No idea," I said, "you wanted to see the pretty flowers, didn't you? Well, go ahead, look at them, there are masses over there."

But Louise said she couldn't care less about our flowers and they were a rotten lot of flowers. I wanted to punch Louise's nose, but I didn't, because the living room window looks out on the yard and both our moms were in the living room.

"Well, I haven't got any toys down here," I said, "only my soccer ball in the garage." Louise thought that was a good idea. We went to get the soccer ball, and I felt very embarrassed, I was dead scared some of my friends might see me playing with a girl.

"You stand in between those trees," said Louise, "and I'll shoot at goal and you try to keep it out." That really made me laugh, and then Louise took this great long run and wham! it was a great shot, right into goal! I couldn't begin to stop it, and the ball broke the garage window.

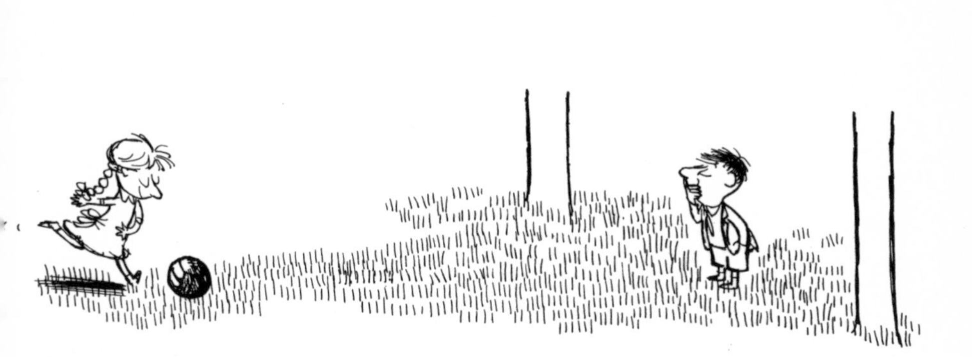

Our moms came running out of the house, and my mom saw the garage window and she grasped the situation in a flash. "Nicholas!" she said, "you ought to look after your guests and not play rough games with them, especially when they're as nice as Louise!" I looked at Louise. She was strolling round the garden smelling the begonias.

I didn't get any dessert at suppertime, but I didn't mind. Louise is great! We'll get married when we're grown up.

She kicks a really fantastic goal!

The Senator's Visit

We were all told to go down to the playground, and the Principal came to speak to us. "Now, children," he said, "I am pleased to tell you that when he passes through our city the Senator himself is going to pay this school the honor of a visit. You may be aware that the Senator is an alumnus of the school. He is an example to you all, an example which proves that if you work hard you can aspire to the highest office! I want the Senator to get a welcome he will never forget, and I am counting on you all to help me." And he sent Matthew and Jeremy to stand in the corner because they were fighting.

After that the Principal called a meeting of all the teachers and he told them about the marvelous ideas he had for welcoming the Senator. For a start, we were going to sing *La Marseillaise*, and then three of the smallest boys would come up to the front with flowers and give them to the Senator. The Principal really does have some great ideas and I'm sure the Senator will be surprised to get flowers, he'll never be expecting that. Our own teacher was looking rather worried, I can't think why. She seems to be all wound up these days.

The Principal said we would begin rehearsing at once, and we thought that was great, because it meant missing lessons. Miss Venables, the music teacher, got us to sing *La Marseillaise*.

She said it wasn't all that good, but we made a fine lot of noise all the same. I suppose our class did get a bit ahead of the big boys; they'd only got to the glory bit by the time we'd reached the end, except for Rufus, that is, who didn't know the words and was going, "La, la, la," and Alec wasn't singing at all because he was in the middle of eating a croissant. Miss Venables waved her arms at us to make us stop, but instead of telling off the big boys for getting left behind she told *us* off, which wasn't fair, because we'd won. Perhaps what really annoyed Miss Venables was the way Rufus was still going, "La, la, la", because he sings with his eyes closed so he hadn't seen he was supposed to stop. Our teacher had a word with the Principal and Miss Venables and then the Principal told us that only the big boys would sing, and we little ones would pretend. So we tried it that way, and it was OK, but there wasn't half as much noise, and the Principal told Alec there was no need to make those faces when you were only pretending to sing and Alec said he wasn't pretending to sing, he was chewing, and the Principal sighed, heavily.

"Right," said the Principal, "now, after *La Marseillaise* we'll have three of the little ones come up to the front." The Principal looked at us and then he picked Eddie, Cuthbert who is top of the class and teacher's pet and me. "A pity there aren't any girls," said the Principal. "We could have dressed them in red, white and blue, or put bows of ribbon in their hair; that's what people sometimes do, and it looks very good."

"Just you try putting a bow in *my* hair!" said Eddie. The Principal turned his head sharply and looked at Eddie with one eye very wide and one very narrow, because he'd brought his eyebrow right down close to it.

"What was that?" asked the Principal, and our teacher said, very quickly, "Oh, nothing, Eddie just coughed."

"Please, miss, no he didn't," said Cuthbert. "I heard what he said, he said ..." But our teacher didn't let him finish, she said she hadn't requested any information from *him*.

"That's right, you sappy little sneak, no one asked *you*," said Eddie. Cuthbert burst into tears and started sobbing that nobody loved him and he was very unhappy and he felt sick and he was going to tell his father and then we'd see, and our teacher told Eddie not to speak without her permission and the Principal passed his hand over his face as if he was wiping it and he asked our teacher whether, if this interesting little conversation was now over, he might be allowed to continue? Our teacher went red in the face, which made her look nice, she's nearly as pretty as Mom, though it's more often Dad who goes red in the face at home.

"Very well," said the Principal. "These three little boys come up to the Senator and give him some flowers. I need something looking like bunches of flowers to rehearse with." Old Spuds, who is one of the masters, said, "I know, sir! I'll be back in a minute!" and he hurried off and came back with three feather dusters. The Principal looked a bit surprised and then he said well, he supposed they'd do for a rehearsal, after all. Old Spuds gave Eddie and Cuthbert and me a feather duster each. "Now, children," said the Principal, "let's pretend that I am the Senator. You come forward and each of you gives me a feather duster." We did what the Principal said and gave him the feather dusters. The Principal was standing there holding the feather dusters and suddenly he got cross.

"You there!" he said, looking at Geoffrey. "I saw you

laughing. Perhaps you'd like to tell us what's so funny, so we can all enjoy the joke!"

"It was what you said, sir!" said Geoffrey. "About putting bows in Nicholas's and Eddie's and silly lame old Cuthbert's hair! That's what made me laugh."

"Want a punch on the nose?" asked Eddie.

"Hear, hear!" I said, and Geoffrey whacked me. We started fighting, and the others joined in too, all except Cuthbert who was rolling about on the ground shouting that he wasn't silly or lame and no one loved him and his father would complain to the Senator. The Principal waved his feather dusters about and shouted, "Stop it! Stop it at once!" Everyone was running about all over the place and Miss Venables felt sick and it was really fantastic!

When the Senator came next day everything went off OK, only we didn't see it, because we'd been shut in the school laundry and even if the Senator had wanted to see us he couldn't have done because the door was locked.

The Principal does get some funny ideas!

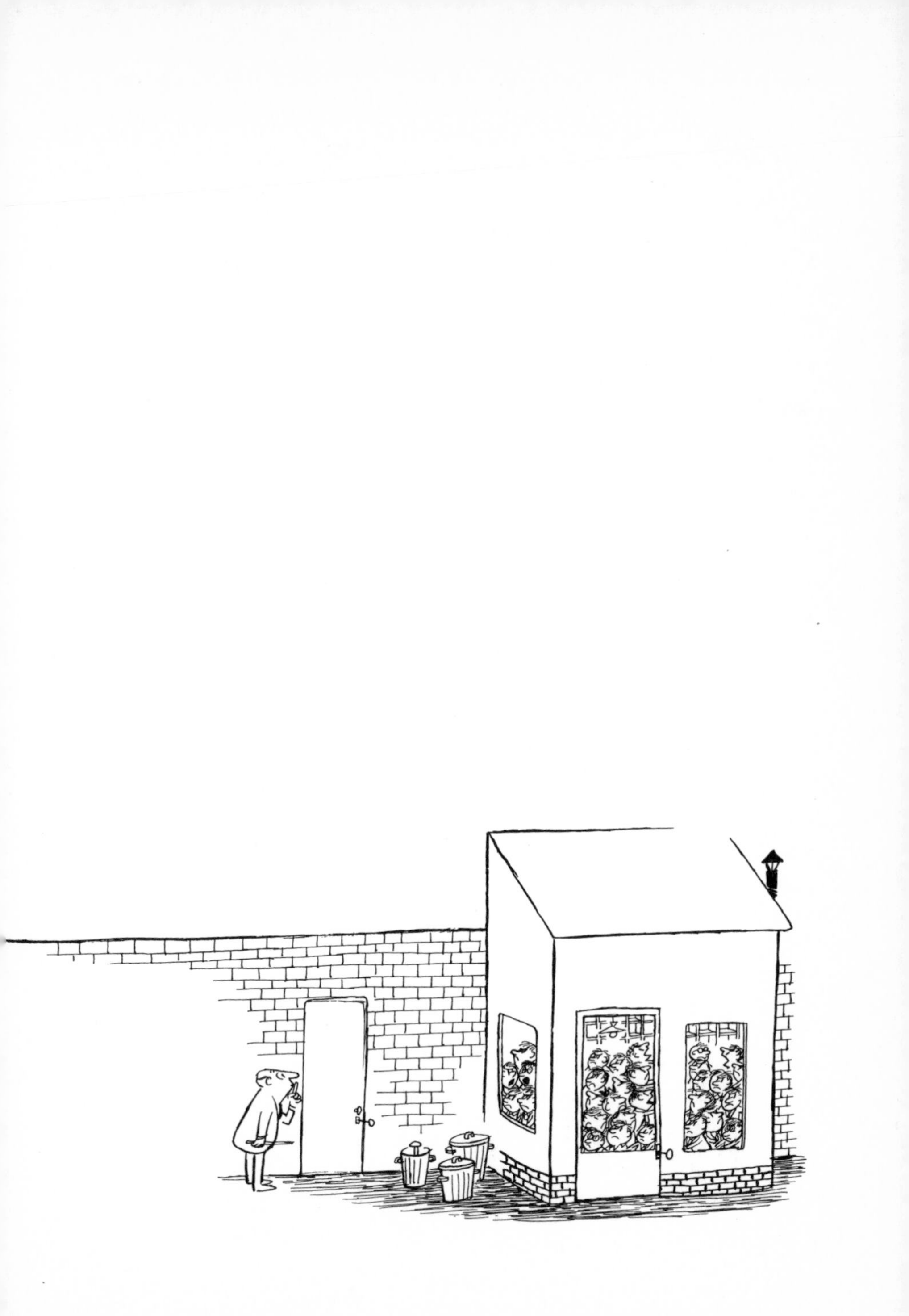

The Cigar

I was out in the yard, doing nothing, when Alec came along and asked me what I was doing and I said, "Nothing."

So Alec said, "You come with me, I've got something to show you. We'll have fun!" I went with Alec, because we do have a lot of fun together. I forget if I told you before, but Alec is my friend who is very fat and eats all the time. Though he wasn't eating at the moment, he had his hand in his pocket and as we walked along the road he kept looking behind him as if he thought he might be being followed.

"What are you going to show me, Alec?" I asked.

"Wait a moment," he said.

Finally, when we were round the corner, Alec took a cigar out of his pocket. "Look at that!" he told me. "It's a real one, not a chocolate cigar." He didn't need to tell me it wasn't a chocolate cigar because if it *had* been a chocolate cigar Alec would have eaten it instead of showing it to me.

I was a bit disappointed. Alec had said we'd have fun. "Well, what do we do with this cigar?" I asked.

"What a ridiculous question!" said Alec. "Smoke it, of course!"

I wasn't all that sure smoking the cigar was a good idea, and I had a feeling Mom and Dad wouldn't like it, but Alec asked me whether my mom and dad had ever told me *not* to smoke this cigar? I thought about it, and I had to admit that Mom and Dad had told me not to draw pictures on the walls of my room, not to speak without being spoken to at meals when we had guests, not to fill the bath to play with my boat, not to eat cookies just before dinner, not to slam the door, not to pick my nose and not to say rude words, but Mom and Dad had never said anything about not smoking this cigar.

"See?" said Alec. "Anyway, just to make sure there isn't any trouble we'll go and hide somewhere we can smoke it in peace." I suggested the vacant lot not far from our house. Dad never goes there. Alec thought that was a good idea, and we were just going to get through the fence into the vacant lot when Alec struck his forehead.

"Have you got a light?" he asked, and I said no. "Then how are we going to smoke the cigar?" he asked. I said we could ask someone in the street for a light. I've seen my dad do that and it's ever so funny because the other man always tries to use his lighter, and he can't because of the wind, so then he offers Dad his own cigarette and Dad presses the lighted end against the end of his cigarette, and the other man's cigarette gets all messed up and the other man isn't very pleased. But Alec said I must be off my head and no one would give us a light in the street because we were too small. It was a pity; I'd have liked messing up someone's cigarette with our big cigar.

"Well, we could go to the smoke shop and buy some matches," I said.

"Got any money?" asked Alec. I said we could club together like we did at the end of the year at school to buy a present for the teacher. Alec got annoyed and said he'd provided the cigar, so it was only fair for me to buy the matches.

"Did you buy the cigar, then?" I asked.

"No," said Alec, "I found it in my dad's desk drawer, and since my dad isn't smoking it, it's no loss to him and he'll never even miss it."

"Well, if you didn't buy the cigar there's no reason why I should buy the matches," I said. But in the end I said all right, I would, so long as Alec went into the smoke shop with me because I was scared to go in alone.

We went into the smoke shop and the lady there said, "Well, what do you want, sweeties?"

"Some matches," I said, and Alec added, "For our dads," only that wasn't very clever, because the lady got suspicious and she said we oughtn't to play with matches and she wouldn't sell us any, and we were little rascals. I liked it better before, when we were sweeties.

We left the smoke shop feeling very mad. It's tricky, smoking

a cigar when you're only little. "I've got a cousin in the Boy Scouts," said Alec. "He said they taught him to make a spark by rubbing sticks together. If we were Scouts we'd know how to smoke this cigar." I didn't realize they taught you that kind of thing in the Scouts, but you shouldn't really believe everything Alec says. Personally *I've* never seen a Boy Scout smoking a cigar.

"I'm fed up with your silly old cigar," I told Alec. "I'm going home."

Alec said, "OK, anyway I'm beginning to feel hungry and I don't want to be late for snack time because there's doughnuts." And then all of a sudden we saw a box of matches lying on the pavement! We picked it up at once and there was one match left. Alec was so excited he forgot about the doughnuts, which shows you he was very excited indeed, to forget a thing like that. "Come on, quick! The vacant lot!" said Alec.

We ran off, and we got through the fence at the place where there's a plank missing. The vacant lot is a fantastic place. We often go there to play. It's got all sorts of things: grass, mud, paving stones, old crates, empty cans, cats and best of all, a car! An old car, of course, without any wheels or engine or doors, but we have a great time in it, we go brrrooom, brrrooom! and we play at buses too, ding, ding, last stop! It's terrific.

"Let's go and smoke in the car," said Alec. We got in and when we sat down the springs of the seats made a funny noise, like Grandpa's old chair at Granny's house, the one she won't have put right because it reminds her of Grandpa.

Alec bit the end of the cigar and spat it out. He told me he'd seen them do that in a gangster movie. And then we took care not to waste the match, and everything went fine. Since it was Alec's cigar he had first go, and he inhaled, making a lot of noise, and there was masses of smoke. The first taste seemed to surprise Alec; it made him cough and he passed me the cigar. I inhaled too, and I have to admit I didn't like it all that much and it made me cough as well. "You just don't know how," said Alec. "Watch me! The smoke comes out through your nose." And Alec took the cigar and tried to make the smoke come out through his nose, and it made him cough like crazy. I had another go, and I did better, only the smoke stung my eyes. We were having a lot of fun.

We were still sharing the cigar when Alec said, "That's funny, I don't feel hungry any more." He was all green, and suddenly he was really sick to his stomach. We threw the cigar away, and my head was going round and round and I felt like

crying. "I'm going home to my mommy," said Alec, and he went away clutching his belly. I don't think he wanted doughnuts at snack time any more.

I went home too. Things weren't too good. Dad was in the living room smoking his pipe and Mom was knitting and I was sick to my stomach. Mom was very worried, she asked me what was wrong with me, I told her it was the smoke but I didn't manage to explain about the cigar because I threw up some more. "There, you see?" Mom said to Dad. "I always told you that pipe of yours made the place reek!" And ever since I smoked that cigar Dad hasn't been allowed to smoke his pipe in the house.

Hop o' my Thumb

Our teacher told us that the Principal was leaving, he was going to retire. We've been getting some fantastic celebrations ready at school, it's going to be just like Graduation and all the mothers and fathers will come, and there'll be chairs in the Auditorium, and armchairs for the Principal and the teachers, and decorations and a platform for the entertainment, which will be given by us boys.

Each class is doing something. The big ones are going to do gymnastics, they all climb on top of each other and the one on top waves a little flag and the audience clap. They did that last year for Graduation and it was absolutely great, though right at the end the flag bit didn't quite work out because they fell down before they could wave it. The class next above us is going to do folk-dancing, all dressed up in peasant costumes with clogs, and they stand in a circle and stomp around the platform in their clogs, only instead of waving a flag they wave hankies and shout "Yoohoo!" They did that last year too; it wasn't as good as the gymnastics display but they didn't fall down. Another class is singing *Frère Jacques* and an alumnus of the school is going to make a speech of congratulations and tell us it was all because of the Principal's good advice he grew to manhood and got to be Town Councilman.

Our part of the entertainment was going to be great. Our teacher told us we were going to act a play – a real play like in the theatre and on Matthew's television because my dad still won't buy us one.

The play is called *Hop o' my Thumb and Puss in Boots*, and we had our first rehearsal at school today. Our teacher was giving out the parts. Geoffrey came dressed up as a cowboy just in case, his dad is very rich and gives him lots of things, but our teacher wasn't all that thrilled with Geoffrey's outfit. "Geoffrey, I've already told you I don't like you coming to school in fancy dress," she said. "Anyway, there aren't any cowboys in this play."

"No cowboys?" said Geoffrey. "What a lousy play!" and the teacher made him stand in the corner.

The play has a very complicated story and I didn't understand it too well when our teacher explained it. I know there's Hop o' my Thumb looking for his brothers and he meets Puss in Boots and there's the Marquis of Carabas and an ogre who wants to eat Hop o' my Thumb's brothers and Puss in Boots helps Hop o' my Thumb and the ogre gets beaten and he turns nice and I think at the end he doesn't eat Hop o' my Thumb's brothers after all and everyone is happy and they have something else to eat instead.

"Now then," said our teacher, "who will be Hop o' my Thumb?"

"Me, miss," said Cuthbert. "It's the main part and I'm top of the class." Which is true, Cuthbert really is top of the class and teacher's pet and a wet blanket who's always crying and he wears glasses and you can't whack him because of the glasses.

"You've got a lot of nerve!" said Eddie. "Watching you act Hop o' my Thumb will be like watching me do embroidery." And Cuthbert started to cry and our teacher sent Eddie to stand in the corner along with Geoffrey.

"Now I want an ogre," said our teacher. "The ogre who wants to eat Hop o' my Thumb." I suggested Alec for the ogre, because he's so fat and he eats all the time. But Alec didn't like that idea, he looked at Cuthbert and he said, "I'm not eating him!" It's the first time I ever knew Alec not to want to eat something, but I suppose the idea of eating Cuthbert isn't exactly appetizing. Cuthbert was upset because Alec didn't want to eat him.

"Take that back or I'll tell my parents and get you expelled!" Cuthbert shouted.

"Silence!" shouted our teacher. "Alec, you can be the crowd of villagers, and you can be prompter too and whisper the words to your friends during the performance." Alec liked the idea of prompting us, like when we're called up to the blackboard to answer questions, he took a cookie out of his pocket and put it in his mouth and said, "Right on!"

"What an expression!" said our teacher. "Please speak correctly!"

"Right on, miss," said Alec, and our teacher sighed, deeply. She does look really tired these days.

First choice for Puss in Boots was Max. Our teacher told him he'd have a lovely costume, with a sword and whiskers and a tail; Max liked the idea of the lovely costume and the whiskers and specially the sword, but he was dead against having any tail.

"I'd look like a monkey!" he said.

"Well, that won't be anything new," said Jeremy, and Max kicked Jeremy, and Jeremy whacked Max, and the teacher put them both in the corner and told me I would be Puss in Boots and if I didn't like it that was just too bad, because she was getting tired of the lot of us and she felt really sorry for our parents who had the job of bringing us up and if we carried on like this we would finish up in jail and she was sorry for the guards too.

After Rufus had been cast as the ogre and Matthew as the Marquis of Carabas, our teacher gave us some typewritten sheets of paper with the words we had to say. She realized there were lots of people standing in the corner by now, so she told them to come back and help Alec be the crowd of villagers. Alec wasn't too pleased, he wanted to be the crowd all on his own, but our teacher told him to be quiet. "Right, let's start," said our teacher. "Read your parts carefully. Cuthbert, this is what you do: you come on stage, you're in despair, it's the middle of the forest and you're looking for your brothers. Then you meet Nicholas, who is Puss in Boots. Then the rest of you in the crowd all say together, 'Why, that's Hop o' my Thumb and Puss in Boots!' Off you go!"

We went and stood in front of the blackboard. I'd stuck a ruler in my belt to pretend it was the sword and Cuthbert began to read his part. "My brothers," he said, "oh, where are my poor brothers?"

"My brothers," shouted Alec, "oh, where are my poor brothers?"

"Whatever do you think you are doing, Alec?" asked our teacher.

"I'm the prompter so I'm prompting, that's all," said Alec.

"Please, miss," said Cuthbert, "when Alec prompts he blows cookie crumbs all over my glasses so I can't see and I'm going to tell my parents!" And Cuthbert took off his glasses to wipe them, so Alec seized the opportunity and whacked him.

"Go on, punch his nose!" shouted Eddie. Cuthbert started howling and crying. He said he was dreadfully unhappy and we wanted to kill him, and he rolled around on the floor. Max, Jeremy and Geoffrey started being the crowd and shouting, "Why, it's Hop o' my Thumb and Puss in Boots!" I was fighting Rufus; I had my ruler and he had a penholder, and the rehearsal was going brilliantly when all of a sudden our teacher shouted, "That will do! Go back to your seats! We will not be acting this play at the celebrations after all. I'm not letting the Principal see a performance like this!"

We all stood there with our jaws dropping.

It's the first time we ever heard our teacher say she was going to give the Principal a punishment.

ALIMENT

The Bike

My dad didn't want to buy me a bike. He was always saying that children are so careless and they will try to do stunt riding and then they break their bikes and hurt themselves. I was always telling Dad that I'd be very careful and then I cried and then I sulked and then I said I was going to run away from home and in the end Dad said I could have a bike if I came in the top ten in the math test.

So I was very pleased when I got home from school yesterday because I'd come tenth in the test. When Dad heard he looked awfully surprised and said, "Well, imagine that!" and Mom hugged me and said Dad would go right out and buy me a beautiful bike straight away and it was very good to do so well on the math test. Actually I was lucky really, because there were only eleven of us doing the test, all the rest of the class was away with colds, and the eleventh was Matthew who always comes last anyway, but it didn't matter for him because he's got a bike already.

When I got home today I found Mom and Dad waiting for me in the yard with big smiles all over their faces.

"We've got a surprise for our big boy!" said Mom, and her eyes were twinkling, and Dad went into the garage and I bet you'll never guess what he came out with: a bike! A shiny red and silver bike with a bicycle light and a bell. It was great! I ran to hug Mom and hug Dad and hug the bike.

"You must promise to be careful," Dad said. "No stunt riding, remember!" I promised, and then Mom hugged me again and said I was her own big boy and she was going to make chocolate mousse for dessert and she went inside. My mom and dad are fantastic!

Dad stayed out in the garden with me. "Did you know I used to be a top-ranking cyclist?" he asked me. "I might have turned professional if I hadn't met your mother." Actually I didn't know. I knew that Dad had been a top-ranking soccer player and rugby football player and swimmer and boxer, but the cycling was a new one on me. "Here, I'll show you," said Dad, and he got on my bike and started riding round the garden. Of course the bike was too small for Dad and he had trouble with his knees which were somewhere up by his face, but he managed.

"Good heavens! That is one of the weirdest sights I have been privileged to behold since last I set eyes on you, my friend!" said Mr. Billings, looking across the garden hedge. Mr. Billings is our neighbor and he and Dad like to annoy each other.

"You be quiet," said Dad, "you don't know the first thing about cycling!"

"Oh, don't I?" said Mr. Billings. "Let me tell you, you poor ignoramus, I was county amateur champion, and if I hadn't met my wife I'd have turned professional."

"You, professional?" said Dad. "Don't make me laugh! You could hardly keep your balance on a tricycle!" Mr. Billings didn't seem to like that.

"I'll show you!" he said, and he jumped over the hedge.

"Give me that bike," he said, grabbing the handlebars, but Dad wasn't letting go of the bike.

"No one asked you in here, Billings," said Dad, "why don't you push off home?"

"Afraid I'll show you up in front of your unfortunate child, eh?" asked Mr. Billings.

"Oh, shut up, you really are the pits!" said Dad, and he tore the handlebars out of Mr. Billings's hands and started riding round the yard again.

"Utterly ridiculous!" said Mr. Billings.

"You needn't think you can get on my last nerve," said Dad. "You're just envious."

I ran after Dad and asked if I could have a go on my bike, but he wasn't listening, because Mr. Billings had started roaring with laughter as he watched Dad, and Dad skidded into the begonias. "Why are you laughing in that silly way?" asked Dad.

"Can I have a go now?" I asked.

"I'm laughing because I feel like laughing," said Mr. Billings.

"It *is* my bike," I said.

"You're out of your mind, my friend!" said Dad.

"Oh, I am, am I?" said Mr. Billings.

"Yes, you are!" said Dad. Then Mr. Billings went up to Dad and pushed him and Dad and my bike fell into the begonias.

"My bike!" I shouted. Dad got up and he pushed Mr. Billings and Mr. Billings fell over too, saying, "Just you do that again!"

When they'd finished pushing each other about, Mr. Billings said, "I've got an idea. We'll race each other round the block by the clock and see who makes the fastest time!"

"Certainly not," said Dad. "I forbid you to ride Nicholas's bike. Anyway you're so fat you'd break it."

"Scared, eh?" said Mr. Billings.

"Scared? Me?" said Dad. "I'll show you!" And Dad took the bike and went out into the road. Mr. Billings and I followed him. I was beginning to get really annoyed, I hadn't even had one go on my bike yet!

"Right," said Dad, "we each ride round the block and time it, and the winner is champion. As far as I'm concerned it's only a formality; I know the winner already."

"Glad to see you admit defeat," said Mr. Billings.

"What about me?" I asked. Dad turned to me, rather surprised, as if he'd forgotten I was there.

"You?" said Dad. "You... er, well, you can be the timekeeper. Mr. Billings will give you his watch." But Mr. Billings didn't want to give me his watch because he said children were always breaking things, so Dad told him how mean he was and he gave me his own watch which is a super watch with a second hand which goes round very fast but I'd really rather have had my bike.

Dad and Mr. Billings drew straws and Mr. Billings had first go. He actually *is* rather fat, so you could hardly see the bike, and people in the road turned to look and laughed at him. He wasn't going very fast, and then he turned the corner and disappeared. When we saw him coming back round the other corner he was red in the face and his tongue was hanging out and he was riding in zigzags.

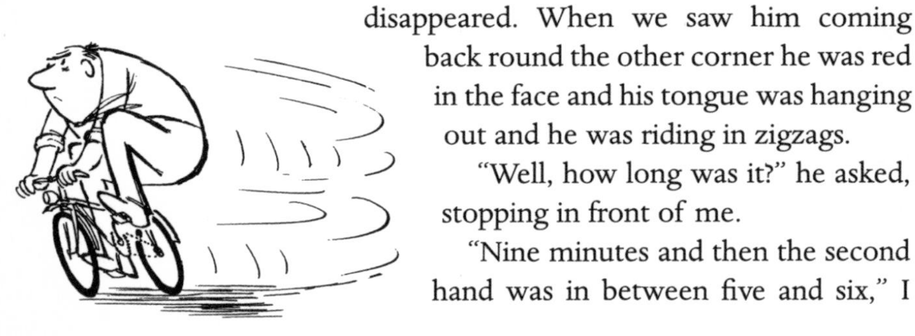

"Well, how long was it?" he asked, stopping in front of me.

"Nine minutes and then the second hand was in between five and six," I said. Dad roared with laughter. "Well, old man," he said, "it'd take you all of six months to do the *Tour de France*."

"Why don't you try to do better instead of indulging in childish jokes?" said Mr. Billings, who was having trouble with his breathing. Dad took the bike and started off.

We waited. Mr. Billings was getting his breath back and I was looking at the watch. I wanted Dad to win, of course, but the hands of the watch kept going round and it was nine minutes and then almost at once it was ten minutes. "I've won! I'm the champion!" cried Mr. Billings.

Fifteen minutes later there was still no sign of Dad.

"That's funny," said Mr. Billings. "Perhaps we ought to go and see what's up." Then we saw Dad coming. On foot. He'd torn his pants, he was pressing a hankie to his nose and carrying the bike in his other hand. Its handlebars were all crossways, its wheels were twisted and the light was broken.

"Ran into a garbage can," said Dad.

Next day I was telling Matthew about it at playtime, and he

told me almost exactly the same thing happened to him with *his* first bike.

"Dads – they're all the same," said Matthew. "They're so careless, and if you don't watch out they go breaking people's bikes and hurting themselves."

I am Sick

I felt fine yesterday; you can tell I did, because I ate a whole lot of caramels and candies and cakes and fries and ice cream, and then in the middle of the night, I can't think why, I was very sick, just like that.

The doctor came this morning. I cried when he walked into my room but more from habit than anything else, because I know the doctor very well and he's really nice. And I like it when he puts his head down on my chest, because the top of it is all bald and shiny and I can see it right under my nose and it's funny. The doctor didn't stay long, he gave me a little pat on the cheek and told Mom, "Put him on an invalid diet and make sure he stays in bed and rests." Then he left.

Mom said, "Well, you heard what the doctor said. I hope you're going to be very good and obedient." I told Mom she didn't need to worry, and she didn't either. I'm very fond of my mom and I always do what she says. It's best to do what she says, or there's trouble.

I got a book and started to read, it was a book full of pictures all about a little bear getting lost in the forest where there are hunters around. I'd really rather have cowboy books, but every birthday Auntie Pauline gives me books about little bears and little rabbits and little cats, all sorts of little animals.

I suppose Auntie Pauline must be fond of little animals.

I was just reading the bit where the big bad wolf was going to eat up the little bear when Mom came in with Alec. Alec is my fat friend who's always eating. "Look Nicholas," said Mom, "here's your little friend Alec come to see you. Isn't that nice of him?"

"Hi, Alec," I said. "It's great to see you!" Mom was just beginning to tell me "great" was a word I used far too much when she spotted the box Alec was carrying.

"What's in there, Alec?" she asked.

"Chocolates," said Alec. So then Mom said it was very kind of Alec, but she didn't want me to have any chocolates because I was on an invalid diet. Alec told Mom the chocolates weren't for me, he'd brought them to eat himself and if I wanted chocolates I'd just have to go and buy my own, so there. Mom gave Alec a rather surprised look, then she sighed and she went out telling us to be good boys. Alec sat down beside my bed and he looked at me without saying anything and he ate his chocolates. I felt terribly envious.

"Hey, Alec, can I have one of your chocolates?" I said.

"You're supposed to be sick, aren't you?" said Alec.

"I thought you were great, Alec, but now I don't think you're great at all!" I told him. Alec said "great" was a word I used far too much and he put two chocolates in his mouth at the same time and then we had a fight.

Mom came running in and she wasn't pleased. She separated us, and told us off, and then she sent Alec home. I was sorry Alec had to go, we were having a lot of fun, but I could see it was no use arguing with Mom because she really didn't look one little bit pleased. Alec shook hands and said goodbye and he left. I like Alec, he's OK.

When Mom looked at my bed she hit the roof. Well, while Alec and I were fighting I suppose we *did* get some of the chocolates squashed on the sheets, and there was chocolate on my pyjamas and in my hair too. Mom said this was really too much, and she changed my sheets and took me into the bathroom and sponged me with eau de Cologne and gave me clean pyjamas, the blue stripy ones. After that Mom put me back to bed and told me not to bother her any more. So I was on my own again and I went back to reading my book, the one about the little bear. It seems the big bad wolf didn't get the little bear because a huntsman had killed the big bad wolf, but now there was a lion wanting to eat the little bear who didn't see the lion because he was eating some honey. All this about eating made me feel hungrier and hungrier. I thought of calling Mom, but she'd told me not to bother her and I didn't want her to tell me off again, so I got up

and went to see if there was anything nice to eat in the fridge.

There were lots of nice things to eat in the fridge. My mom is a good cook. I took a chicken leg, because I like cold chicken, and a piece of cream sponge cake and a bottle of milk. Then I heard someone shout, "Nicholas!" right behind me. I was so startled that I dropped the lot. It was Mom coming into the kitchen and I don't suppose she was expecting to find me there. I started crying, to be on the safe side, because Mom was looking very cross indeed, so then Mom didn't say anything, she took me into the bathroom and sponged me with eau de Cologne and gave me clean pyjamas because the ones I was wearing had got milk and cream cake all over them. Mom gave me my red check pyjamas and sent me straight off to bed because she had to clean up the kitchen.

Back in bed I didn't feel like going on with my book about the little bear that everyone wanted to eat. I'd had about enough of that silly bear making me do all the wrong things. But it was no fun just staying there with nothing to do, so I decided to draw. I went to look in Dad's desk for the things I needed. I wasn't going to take any of the nice clean sheets of white paper with Dad's name in shiny letters in the corner, because I knew I'd get told off for that, so I took some bits of paper which already had writing on one side so I was sure they weren't any more use. And I took Dad's old fountain pen too.

I darted back to my room and got into bed, and started drawing. I drew some fabulous things: warships firing guns at planes which were exploding in the sky, and castles with lots of people attacking them and lots of other people throwing things down on their heads to try and stop them. I'd been perfectly quiet for a bit, so Mom came to see what was going on and she started shouting all over again. Well, I must admit Dad's pen *was* leaking a bit, that's why Dad doesn't use it any more. It comes in useful for drawing explosions, but I'd got ink everywhere, on the sheets and the bedspread too. Mom was mad and she didn't like me using that paper with writing on because it turned out the things written on the other side of my drawing were something important of Dad's.

Mom made me get up, and she changed the sheets, she took me into the bathroom and scrubbed me with pumice stone and sponged me with what was left at the bottom of the eau de Cologne bottle, and she put one of Dad's old shirts on me instead of pyjamas because I didn't have any clean pyjamas left.

In the evening the doctor came to listen to my chest, and I put out my tongue at him, he gave me a little pat on the cheek and told me I was better now and I could get up.

But we do seem to be awfully unhealthy in our family today. The doctor said Mom was looking poorly now, and he told her to go to bed and put herself on an invalid diet.

SCHOOL

Having Fun

This afternoon I ran into Alec on my way to school and he said, "Suppose we play hooky?" I told him that would be naughty and our teacher wouldn't be pleased, and Dad had told me you had to work if you wanted to get on in life and be an air force man, and Mom would be sad and it was wicked to tell lies. Alec reminded me it was math this afternoon, so I said, "OK," and we didn't go to school.

We ran off in the opposite direction instead. Alec started puffing and blowing and he couldn't keep up. I ought to mention that Alec is my fat friend who's always eating, so of course he isn't too good at running, and I happen to be really great at the forty meters sprint, which is the length of the school playground.

"Hurry up, Alec!" I said.

"I can't!" said Alec. And he did a lot more puffing and then stopped entirely. I told him it was no good staying here, or our moms and dads might see us and not let us have any dessert, and then there were school inspectors who'd put us in jail and keep us on bread and water. When Alec heard that it made him much braver and he started running so fast I could hardly keep up myself.

We stopped a long way off, just past the nice grocery store

where Mom buys the strawberry jelly I like. "We'll be safe here," said Alec, and he took some cookies out of his pocket and started eating them because, he told me, running right after lunch like that had made him hungry.

"This is a good idea of yours, Alec!" I said. "When I think of the others doing math at school I could laugh my head off!"

"Me too," said Alec, so we laughed. When we'd finished laughing I asked Alec what we were going to do now.

"No idea," said Alec. "We could go to the movies." That was a great idea too, only we didn't have any money. When we turned out our pockets we found string, marbles, two elastic bands and some crumbs. The crumbs were in Alec's pocket and he ate them.

"Oh well," I said, "never mind, even if we can't go to the movies the others would rather be here with us!"

"You bet!" said Alec. "Anyway, I wasn't really all that excited to see *The Sheriff's Revenge*."

"Nor me," I said. "I mean, it's only a Western." And we walked past the movie theater to look at the posters outside. There was a cartoon on too.

"Suppose we went to the park?" I said. "We could make a ball out of old paper and have a game." Alec said that wasn't a bad idea, only there was a man in charge of the park and if he saw us he'd ask us why we weren't at school and he'd take us away and lock us in a dungeon and keep us on bread and water. Just thinking of it made Alec feel hungry, and he got a cheese sandwich out of his book bag. We went on walking down the road, and when Alec had finished his sandwich he said, "Well, the others at school aren't having any fun, are they?"

"No way," I said, "and anyway it's too late to go now, we'd get punished."

We looked in the store windows. Alec told me what all the things in the butcher's window were, and then we went to make faces in the mirrors which are in the window of the store selling perfume and stuff, but we went away again because we saw the people inside the store looking at us and they seemed rather surprised. We looked at the clocks in the jewelry store window and it was still really early.

"Great!" I said. "Plenty of time for us to have fun before we go home."

We were beginning to feel tired with all this walking, so then Alec suggested going to the vacant lot, there's no one around there and you can sit down. The vacant lot is really good. We had fun throwing stones at the empty tin cans. Then we got tired of throwing stones so we sat down and Alec started on a ham sandwich out of his book bag. It was his last sandwich.

"They must be in the middle of doing problems at school," said Alec.

"No, they aren't," I said. "It'll be playtime by now."

"Huh! You don't really think playtime is any fun, do you?" Alec asked me.

"You bet I don't!" I said, and then

I started to cry. Let's face it, it wasn't all that much fun here all on our own, with nothing to do, and having to hide, and I was right to want to go to school even if it *was* math and if I hadn't gone and met Alec I'd be having playtime now and I'd be playing marbles and cops and robbers and I'm very good at marbles.

"Why are you howling like that?" asked Alec.

I said, "It's all your fault I can't play cops and robbers."

Alec lost his temper. "I didn't *ask* you to come with me," he said, "and what's more if you'd said you wouldn't come I'd have gone to school too so it's your fault."

"Oh, really?" I said to Alec in the sarcastic voice Dad uses to Mr. Billings who lives next door and likes to annoy Dad.

"Yes, really," said Alec, just the same way Mr. Billings says it to Dad, and we had a fight, just like Dad and Mr. Billings.

When we'd finished our fight it started raining, so we went away from the vacant lot because there wasn't anywhere to shelter from the rain, and my mom doesn't like me to stay out in the wet and I almost never disobey my mom.

Alec and I went to stand by the jewelry store window with the clocks in it. It was raining hard and we were all alone there and it wasn't much fun. We waited till it was time to go home.

When I got home Mom said I looked so pale and tired I could stay away from school tomorrow if I liked, and I said no and Mom was very surprised.

The thing is, when Alec and I tell all the others at school tomorrow what fun we had they'll be green with envy!

WHAT'S THIS I HEAR? PLAYING HOOKY?
THAT'S THE BOY WHO DIDN'T GO TO SCHOOL...
WHY DIDN'T YOU GO TO SCHOOL?

Playing with Cuthbert

I wanted to go out and play with our gang, but Mom said no, nothing doing, she didn't care for the little boys I went around with, we were always up to something silly, and anyway I was invited to have tea with Cuthbert who was a nice little boy with such good manners, and it would be a very good thing if I tried to be more like him.

I wasn't so thrilled to go to tea with Cuthbert, or try to be more like him. Cuthbert is top of the class and teacher's pet and a rotten sport but we can't whack him much because of his glasses. I'd rather have gone to the swimming pool with Alec and Geoffrey and Eddie and the rest, but there it was, Mom looked as if she wasn't standing for any nonsense, and anyway I always do what Mom says especially when she looks as if she isn't standing for any nonsense.

Mom made me wash and comb my hair and told me to put on my blue sailor suit with the nice creases in the pants, and my white silk shirt and spotted tie. I had to wear that outfit for my cousin Angela's wedding, the time I threw up after the reception.

"And don't look like that!" said Mom. "You'll have a very nice time playing with Cuthbert, I'm sure." Then we went out. I was scared stiff of meeting the gang. They'd have laughed like a hyena to see me decked out like that!

Cuthbert's mom opened the door. "Oh, isn't he sweet!" she said, and she hugged me and then she called Cuthbert. "Cuthbert! Come along. Here's your little friend Nicholas." So Cuthbert came along, he was all dressed up too, with velvet pants and white socks and funny shiny black sandals. We looked a pair of real nitwits, him and me.

Cuthbert didn't look all that pleased to see me either, he shook my hand and his hand was all limp. "Well, I'll be off," said Mom. "I hope he'll behave, and I'll be back to pick him up at six." And Cuthbert's mom said she was sure we'd play nicely and I'd be very good. Mom gave me a rather worried look and then she went away.

We had tea. That was OK, there was hot chocolate to drink and Jell-O and cake and cookies and we didn't put our elbows on the table. After tea Cuthbert's mom told us to go and have a nice game in Cuthbert's room.

Up in his room Cuthbert started by telling me I mustn't whack him because he wore glasses and if I did he'd start to shout and his mom would have me put in jail. I told him I'd just love to whack him, but I wasn't going to because I'd promised my mom to be good. Cuthbert seemed to like the sound of that, and he said right, we'd play. He got out heaps of books: geography books and science books and math books, and he said we could read and do some problems to pass the time. He told me he knew some brilliant problems about the water from the faucet running into a bath with the plug pulled out so the bath emptied at the same time as it was filling.

That didn't sound a bad idea, and I asked Cuthbert if I could see his bath because it might be fun. Cuthbert looked at me, took off his glasses, wiped them, thought a minute and then told me to come with him.

There was a big bath in the bathroom and I said why didn't we fill it and sail boats on it? Cuthbert said he'd never thought of that, but it was quite a good idea. The bath didn't take long to fill right up to the top (we put the plug in, not like the problem). But then we were stuck because Cuthbert didn't have any boats to sail in it. He explained that he didn't have many toys at all, he mostly had books. But luckily I can make paper boats and we took some pages out of his math book. Of course we tried to be careful so that Cuthbert could stick the pages back in the book afterwards, because it's very naughty to harm a book, a tree or a poor dumb animal.

We had a really great time. Cuthbert swished his arm around in the water to make waves. It was a pity he didn't roll up his shirtsleeves first, and he didn't take off the watch he got for coming first in the last history test we had and now it says twenty past four all the time. After a bit longer, I don't know just how much longer because of the watch not working, we'd had enough of playing boats. Anyway there was water all over the place and we didn't want to make too much mess because there were muddy puddles on the floor and Cuthbert's sandals weren't as shiny as they used to be.

We went back to Cuthbert's room and he showed me his globe, which is a big metal ball on a stand with seas and continents and things on it. Cuthbert explained that it was for learning geography and finding where the different countries were. I knew that already, there's a globe like that at school and our teacher showed us how it works. Cuthbert told me you could unscrew his globe, and then it was like a big ball. I think it was me who got the idea of playing ball with it, only that turned out not to be such a very good idea after all. We did have some fun throwing and catching the globe, but Cuthbert had taken off his glasses so as not to risk breaking them, and he doesn't see very well without his glasses, so he missed the globe and the part with Australia on it hit his mirror and the mirror got broken. Cuthbert put his glasses on again to see what had happened and he was very upset. We put the globe back on its stand and decided to be more careful in case our moms weren't too pleased.

So we looked for something else to do, and Cuthbert told me his dad had given him a chemistry set to help him with science. He showed me the chemistry set; it's awesome. It's a big box full of tubes and funny round bottles and little flasks full of things all different colors, and a spirit burner too. Cuthbert told me you could do some very instructive experiments with this chemistry set.

He started pouring little bits of powder and liquid into the tubes and they changed color and went red or blue and now and then there was a puff of white smoke. It was ever so instructive. I told Cuthbert we ought to try something even more instructive, and he agreed. We took the biggest bottle and tipped all the powders and liquids into it and then we got the spirit burner and heated up the bottle. It was OK to start with; the stuff began frothing up, and then there was some very black smoke. The trouble was the smoke didn't smell too good and it made everything very dirty. When the bottle burst we had to stop the experiment.

Cuthbert started howling that he couldn't see any more, but luckily it was only because the lenses of his glasses were all black, and while he wiped them I opened the window, because the smoke was making us cough. And the froth was making funny noises on the carpet, like boiling water, and the walls were all black and we weren't terribly clean ourselves.

Then Cuthbert's mom came in. For a moment she didn't say anything at all, just opened her eyes and her mouth very wide, and then she started to shout, she took off Cuthbert's glasses and she slapped him, and then she led us off to the bathroom to get washed. When Cuthbert's mom saw the bathroom she wasn't too pleased about that either.

Cuthbert was hanging on to his glasses for dear life, so as not to get slapped again. Cuthbert's mom went off telling me she was going to call my mother and ask her to come and fetch me immediately and she'd never seen anything like it in all her born days and it was absolutely terrible.

Mom did come to fetch me pretty soon, and I was pleased, because I wasn't having so much fun at Cuthbert's house any more, not with his mom carrying on like that. Mom took me home, telling me all the way she supposed I was proud of myself and I wouldn't have any dessert this evening. I must say, that was fair enough, because we did do one or two silly things at Cuthbert's. And actually Mom was right, as usual: I *did* have a nice time playing with Cuthbert. I'd have liked to go and see him again, but it seems that Cuthbert's mom doesn't want him to be friends with me.

Honestly, mothers! I do wish they could make up their minds, you just don't know *who* to play with!

CONCIERG

Mr. Bainbridge and the Fine Weather

I can't make out why Mr. Bainbridge says he doesn't like fine weather. I mean, rain isn't much fun. Not that you can't have *some* fun in the rain. You can walk in the gutter and put your head back and open your mouth to catch raindrops, and it's nice at home because the house is all warm and I can play with my electric trains and Mom makes hot chocolate and cakes. Still, when it rains there isn't any playtime at school because they don't let us out in the playground, and that's why I can't figure Mr. Bainbridge out. The thing is, *he* has a nice time when it's fine, too, because he's on playground duty.

For instance it was very fine today, with lots of sun, and we had a terrific time at playtime, especially because it had been raining nonstop for three days and we had to stay in the classroom. We filed out into the playground, same as usual, and Mr. Bainbridge said, "Dismiss!" and we started having fun.

"Let's play cops and robbers," said Rufus, whose dad is a policeman.

"Don't be so ridiculous," said Eddie, "we're going to play soccer." And they had a fight. Eddie is very strong and he likes to punch his friends' noses, and since Rufus is a friend of his he punched his nose, which Rufus wasn't expecting, so he stepped backwards and bumped into Alec who happened to be eating a jelly sandwich and the sandwich fell on the ground and Alec started yelling. Mr. Bainbridge came running up and separated Eddie and Rufus and sent them to stand in the corner of the playground.

"What about my sandwich?" asked Alec. "Who's giving me compensation for my sandwich?"

"Do you want to go and stand in the corner too?" asked Mr. Bainbridge.

"No, I want my jelly sandwich," said Alec.

Mr. Bainbridge went bright red and he started to breathe heavily through his nose, which he does when he's about to lose his temper, but he couldn't carry on his conversation with Alec because Max and Jeremy were having a fight.

"You cheated! Give me back my marble!" Jeremy was shouting, and he was pulling Max's tie and Max was whacking him.

"What's going on here?" asked Mr. Bainbridge.

"Jeremy's a sore loser, that's what. I can give him a punch on the nose if you like, sir," said Eddie, who had come along to watch. Mr. Bainbridge was rather surprised to see Eddie.

"I thought you were standing in the corner?" he said.

"Oh yes, so I was," said Eddie, and he went back to the corner, and meanwhile Max was going bright red because Jeremy still had hold of his tie, and Mr. Bainbridge sent them both to stand in the corner with the others.

"What about my jelly sandwich, then?" asked Alec, who was eating a jelly sandwich.

"But you're eating one, boy!" said Mr. Bainbridge.

"That's got nothing to do with it!" shouted Alec. "I brought four sandwiches to school!" Mr. Bainbridge didn't have time to lose his temper because our ball hit him on the head, wham!

"Who was that?" shouted Mr. Bainbridge, rubbing his forehead.

"Please, sir, it was Nicholas, I saw him!" said Cuthbert, who is top of the class and teacher's pet and we don't like him too much, in fact he's a nasty little sneak, but he wears glasses so you can't whack him as often as you'd like to.

"You rotten little nitwit!" I shouted. "If you didn't wear glasses, I'd show you!"

Cuthbert started crying and saying he was dreadfully unhappy and he was going to kill himself and then he rolled about on the ground. Mr. Bainbridge asked if it was really me who threw that ball and I said, yes, we were playing ball tag and I'd missed Matthew and it wasn't my fault because I didn't mean to hit you, Mr. Bainbridge.

"I won't have you playing these rough games. I am confiscating that ball," Mr. Bainbridge told me. "As for you, go and stand in the corner!" I told him that was very unfair, and Cuthbert said, "Yah!" and looked very pleased and he went off with his book. Cuthbert doesn't play at playtime, he takes a book and revises. Cuthbert is nuts!

"Well, what about my sandwich? I tell you, playtime's nearly over and I'm going to be minus one sandwich!" said Alec. Mr. Bainbridge started saying something to Alec but he couldn't go on which was a pity because it looked as if what he was about to say might be quite interesting. The reason why he couldn't go on was because Cuthbert was lying on the ground letting out awful yells.

"Now what?" asked Mr. Bainbridge.

"Geoffrey! He pushed me! My glasses! I'm dying!" said Cuthbert, and his voice was like the characters in a movie I saw where there were some people trapped in a submarine which couldn't surface and the people managed to get out but the submarine was totaled.

"Oh no, sir, it wasn't Geoffrey, Cuthbert fell over all by himself, he lost his balance," said Eddie.

"Who asked you to go sticking your nose in?" asked Geoffrey. "No one wants you interfering, I did push Cuthbert, so what?" Mr. Bainbridge started shouting at Eddie to get back in the corner and he told Geoffrey to go with him. And then he picked up Cuthbert, whose nose was bleeding and he was crying, and he took him to the nurse's office and Alec followed talking about his jelly sandwich.

We decided to have a game of soccer, only the trouble was the big boys were already playing soccer in the playground and we don't always get on too well with the big boys and there's often a bit of fighting. And that was what happened now, with two balls and two games all getting mixed up. "Leave that ball alone, you snotty little kid!" said one of the big boys to Rufus. "It's ours!"

"It isn't!" shouted Rufus, and he was right, it wasn't, and one big boy kicked a goal with our ball and the big boy hit Rufus and Rufus kicked the big boy's shin. Fights with the big boys are always like that: they hit us and we kick them. We were really putting all we'd got into it, and everyone was fighting and making no end of noise, but even through the noise we could hear Mr. Bainbridge shouting when he came back from the nurse's office with Cuthbert and Alec.

"Oh, Mr. Bainbridge, they're not in the corner any more!" said Cuthbert. Mr. Bainbridge looked very mad and he ran towards us but he never got there because he slipped on

Alec's jelly sandwich and fell over.

"Oh, thanks very much!" said Alec. "That's right, go trampling all over my jelly sandwich!"

Mr. Bainbridge got up wiping his pants and he had jelly all over his hand. We started fighting again, we were having a fantastic playtime, but Mr. Bainbridge looked at his watch and he went off, limping, to ring the bell. And playtime was over.

While we were getting into line Old Spuds came along. Old Spuds is another teacher and we call him that because he is always saying, "Boy, look me in the eye!" and there are eyes in potatoes so we call him Spuds. It was the big boys who thought of that one.

"Well, how was it, old boy?" asked Spuds.

"Same as usual," said Mr. Bainbridge, "what d'you expect? Personally, I pray daily for rain. My heart really sinks when I get up in the morning and I see it's fine!"

I honestly can't make Mr. Bainbridge out. Imagine not liking fine weather!

Running Away From Home

I'm running away from home! I was playing in the living room, being very good, and just because I'd spilt a bottle of ink on the new carpet Mom came along and told me off. Then I started crying and I told her I was going to run away and she'd be sorry and Mom said, "Good heavens, it's getting late! I must run out and do the shopping," and she went out.

I went up to my room to get the things I'd need for running away from home. I took my book bag, and I packed the little red car Auntie Elizabeth gave me, and the engine of the little clockwork train and the freight car which is the only one I've got left because all the others are broken, and a piece of chocolate I'd saved from tea-time, and I took my piggy bank because you never know, I might need some money, and I set off.

It was a bit of luck Mom was out, because I'm pretty sure she'd have said I mustn't run away from home. Once I was out on the road I started to hurry. I thought, Mom and Dad will be ever so upset, and I will come back later, when they're very, very old, as old as Granny, and I'll be rich, I will have a big plane and a big car and a carpet all my own and I can spill as much ink as I like on it and they'll be terribly pleased to see me.

Hurrying along like this, I found myself outside Alec's house. Alec is my friend who is very fat and who eats all the time, perhaps I may have mentioned him before. Well, Alec was sitting outside his house eating a piece of gingerbread.

"Where are you going?" asked Alec, taking a big bite of the gingerbread.

I explained how I'd run away from home and I asked if he'd like to come too. "And when we come back after years and years and years we'll be very rich," I told him, "We'll have planes and cars and our moms and dads will be so pleased to see us they'll never tell us off any more."

But Alec didn't want to come. "Are you nuts?" he said. "My mom's got beans and sausages for supper, I couldn't possibly come!" So I said goodbye to Alec, and he waved his free hand, the one that wasn't busy stuffing gingerbread into his mouth.

I turned the corner of the road and I stopped for a moment, because Alec had made me feel hungry, so I ate my piece of chocolate, and that gave me strength for the journey. I wanted to go a long, long way away, somewhere Mom and Dad would never find me, like China or Brittany, where we went for our vacation last year and it's really far from our house, the sea is there, and oysters.

But I'd need to buy a car or a plane to go a long way away. I sat down on the side of the road and opened my piggy bank and counted my money. I could see there wasn't enough for a car or a plane, so I went into a bakery and bought myself a chocolate éclair. It was lovely.

When I'd finished the éclair I decided to do the journey on foot, it would take longer but as I didn't have to go home or go to school I had all the time in the world. I hadn't thought about school before, and I told myself that our teacher would say in class tomorrow, "Poor little Nicholas! He's run away from home all by himself, and gone a long way away, and when he comes back he'll be very rich and have a car and a plane," and everyone would be talking about me and they'd be really worried and Alec would be sorry he hadn't come too. It would be great!

I went on walking, but I was beginning to get tired. I wasn't really going very fast, I don't have very long legs, not like my friend Max, but I couldn't very well ask Max to lend me his legs. That gave me an idea, though; I could ask one of the gang to lend me a bike. I happened to be passing Matthew's house, and Matthew has a super bike, all shiny and yellow. The trouble is, Matthew isn't very fond of lending out his things.

I rang Matthew's bell and he opened the door himself. "Hi, Nicholas," he said. "What do you want?"

"Your bike," I said, and then Matthew slammed the door. I rang the bell again and since Matthew didn't open up I kept

my finger on the button. Somewhere inside the house I heard Matthew's mom shout, "Matthew, go and open the door!" So Matthew did open the door, but he didn't look at all pleased to see me still there.

"Listen, Matthew, I need your bike," I said. "I've run away from home and my mom and dad will be sorry and I'll come back in years and years and years when I'll be very rich and I'll have a car and a plane." Matthew said OK, I could come and see him when I got back and I was very rich and then he'd sell me his bike. That didn't really suit me, but I thought I'd better find some money and then I could buy the bike. Matthew is very fond of money.

So I wondered how to get hold of some money. I couldn't do any work because it was after school, so I thought of selling the toys I had in my book bag, Auntie Elizabeth's car and the clockwork engine with the freight car which is the only one left because the others are all broken. I saw a toy store on the other side of the road and I thought they might be interested in my car and my train in there.

I went into the store and a very nice man smiled and said, "Well, what can I do for you, sonny? Some marbles? A ball?" I told him I didn't want to buy any toys, I wanted to sell some, and I opened my book bag and put the car and train down on the floor in front of the counter. The nice man bent down to look, he seemed rather surprised, and he said, "But I don't buy toys, sonny,

I sell them!" So I asked where he found the toys he sold, because I'd like to know. "But I don't *find* them," he cried. "I buy them."

"Then you can buy mine, can't you?" I told the man.

"But," said the nice man again, "you don't understand. I do buy toys but not from you. I sell them to you; I buy them from the manufacturers and you… that is…" He stopped and then he said, "Well, you'll understand it all later on, when you grow up." Of course the nice man wasn't to know that when I'm grown up I won't be needing any money because I shall be so rich with my car and my plane. I started to cry. The nice man was very upset, and he looked behind the counter and gave me a little car and then he told me I'd better be on my way because it was getting late and he had to close the store, and he found a customer like me very tiring after a hard day's work. So I left the shop with my little train and *two* cars, feeling ever so pleased. He was right about it getting late, it was nearly dark and there wasn't anyone about on the streets and I started to run. And when I got home Mom was mad with me for being late for supper!

So now I've really made up my mind. If that's how they feel, I'm running away from home tomorrow. Mom and Dad will be very sorry and I won't come back for years and years and years and then I'll be rich and I'll have a car and a plane and everything!

Anthea Bell

Anthea Bell was awarded the Independent Foreign Fiction Prize and the Helen and Kurt Wolff Prize (USA) in 2002 for her translation of W.G. Sebald's Austerlitz. *Her many works of translation from French and German (for which she has received several other awards) include the* Nicholas *books and, with Derek Hockridge, the entire* Asterix the Gaul *saga by René Goscinny and Albert Uderzo.*

René Goscinny

René Goscinny is the world-famous writer and creator, along with Albert Uderzo, of the adventures of Asterix the Gaul. Born in Paris in 1926, Goscinny lived in Buenos Aires and New York. He returned to France in the 1950s where he met Jean-Jacques Sempé and they collaborated on picture strips and then stories about Nicholas, the popular French schoolboy. An internationally successful children's author, who also won awards for his animated cartoons, Goscinny died in 1977.

Jean-Jacques Sempé

Jean-Jacques Sempé is one of the most successful cartoonists and illustrators in the world, whose works are featured in countless magazines and newspapers. Born in Bordeaux, France in 1932, Sempé was expelled from school for bad behavior. He enjoyed a variety of jobs, from traveling toothpaste salesman to summer camp worker, before winning an art prize in 1952. Although Sempé was never trained formally as an artist, more than twenty volumes of his drawings have been published, in thirty countries.

Nicholas Again

Watch out for *Nicholas Again*. The adventures of Nicholas and his pals continue in this book, the second in the series, coming soon...

Top row, left to right: Martin (he moved
Bowery, Green

Middle row: Paul Milligan, Joe Millig
Sutherland, Geoffre

Seated: Roberts, Max, Gulliver, Cliff,
Gonzales, Matthew, Al